For nigh unto two years now, this great war, this fight for freedom, hath raged on, with no end in sight. And yet, in the midst of it all, we find life here in our little corner of the world has settled into a calm such as we have not experienced in many years, I fear we must fight off the temptation of complacency. I yearn to be of service to those still held in bondage despite the president's decree of emancipation. No parcels have come to us in over a year, and I suffer with the guilt of knowing we live in comfort and ease while others struggle still under the oppressive yoke of slavery. My dear husband is well aware of my double-minded heart. He tells me to be content rolling bandages and gathering goods for the soldiers and the wounded, that when the Good Lord hath need of us for other tasks, He shall surely let us know.

—Prudence Willard
Marietta, Ohio
April 2, 1863

SECRETS OF WAYFARERS INN

SECRETS OF

WAYFARERS INN

Forget-Me-Nots

TRACEY BATEMAN

New York

SECRETS OF WAYFARERS INN

Forget-Me-Nots

CHAPTER ONE

April 6, 1863

Despite the warmth of the sun shining down on the little spot behind the house, Prudence Willard knew it was likely a foolhardy exercise to plant a garden so early in April. But after such a long, hard winter, she couldn't bear the thought of remaining housebound. With effort, she had convinced her reluctant husband to turn the ground and make it ready for her to plant the vegetables she could already envision adorning her dinner table in a couple of months.

"Thee does know the seeds thee is planting are never going to grow?"

Prudence tossed Jason a cheeky grin and shrugged. "It has been mild for over a week now. The Lord may bless us with warmth from here on out."

With a grin in return, he swiped at her nose with a dirt-smudged finger.

"Jason Willard!" She attempted to sound stern, despite the laughter in her voice. "Thee will pay for that."

He took off as fast as his limping leg would allow, and Prudence deliberately moved slower than she was capable of, though she knew she certainly wasn't fooling him.

Several years had passed since he'd been injured while helping a runaway slave, and he no longer became defensive about his handicap. Still, sparing him humiliation had been her task for so long, she did so instinctively. As instinctively as she protected their four-year-old son, Moses.

For Prudence, the loss of her precious baby girl soon after birth and the heartbreak of losing several babies not fully brought to term had been her cross to carry. Though she praised the Lord for their dear Moses, she had dreamed of being a mother to a brood. But the Lord had other plans for them. By His grace, she and Jason had saved countless, body and soul, from the ravages of slavery.

However, for the past two years, with the war raging in the Southern states, their work in getting slaves to the next station toward freedom was vastly curtailed, and now it had been over a year since a new "package" had arrived. She hated the thought of the hardships people must be enduring in the South, smack in the middle of fighting. Prudence and Jason had discovered that, as difficult as it had been for slaves to escape before the war, the fighting and constant threat of being caught and conscripted into either army kept most of the slaves on the plantations, likely praying for victory for Mr. Lincoln's army.

Beneath the weight of her thoughts, Prudence realized she had stopped running after Jason altogether. He stood a couple of yards away, staring at her with a mixture of compassion and exasperation.

"Thee is thinking about the war again." He closed the distance between them.

She nodded as he wrapped her in his arms and drew her close. A heavy sigh left him, and she knew what he was going to say. "Dear, thy heavenly Father loves His children in bondage even more than we do. They will soon be free."

Enjoying the comfort of his warm body and solid chest, she remained silent, unwilling to ruin the moment for either of them. She longed to explain the disquiet inside of her in a way that would make him understand how utterly useless she'd felt since their calling had apparently come to an end. But a high-pitched scream coming from somewhere at the front of the house made them both jump and take off running. This time, Prudence sprinted ahead of her husband, heedless of his pride as her baby boy cried for his mama.

Prudence reached Moses in only a few seconds, then stopped short at the sight that greeted her. Her heart reached her throat as she froze, staring at a snarling, half-starved bloodhound with its teeth bared at her little boy.

Tess Wallace enjoyed the aroma of her first mug of coffee for the day—fully caffeinated, of course. After all, it was barely six thirty when she left the kitchen, which was filled with the scents of bread dough, bacon, and other tantalizing breakfast foods Winnie had begun to prepare.

She headed toward the office but went past it when she heard the front door open, then close. Curious, she walked to the foyer to find LuAnn unhooking Huck's leash. The former stray ran straight to Tess. She held up her hand and he sat, looking up at her expectantly, tail wagging a hundred beats a minute. With an indulgent smile, Tess bent and scratched the little dog behind his ears.

"He's wet." She glanced at LuAnn as she straightened.

"It's starting to sleet." LuAnn shivered. "*Brr.* He didn't take long out there."

Tess returned her friend's smile. "He's up early today."

Smothering a yawn with the back of her hand, LuAnn nodded. "He heard you leave your room, I think."

"Sorry."

With a little wave, LuAnn looked toward the kitchen. "Winnie's coffee will wake me right up. Do you mind keeping an eye on Huck?"

Tess glanced at the dog, still sitting at her feet, still wagging his tail. "I don't mind, if he doesn't. I'm just going into the office to do my devotions and some paperwork."

"Thanks," LuAnn said. "I'd hate for him to run up and down the stairs this early and risk waking any of the guests. I won't be too long unless Winnie needs help."

"Good luck with that," Tess called after LuAnn as her friend headed toward the kitchen. "She didn't want my help." The inn had been at nearly full capacity over the weekend, and most of the guests would leave today. That meant they would want a final, full breakfast from Winnie's masterful hand before checking out. The dining room would soon be hopping.

With a glance at Huck, she turned and started to walk back toward the office. The dog would follow without a command, so she didn't give one.

Tess wrapped her cold fingers around the mug and allowed it to begin warming her like the first rays of sun on a spring day—not that they'd had much of that over the past week. She heard the distinct sound of pinging against the windows in the foyer and, on a whim, made another detour from her intended destination. She walked toward the front door, with Huck trailing, his doggie nails keeping a steady rhythm on the hardwood floor. Goodness, someone needed to take him to the groomer and get those claws trimmed before he scratched the finish on their beautiful floors. He sat at her feet while she pulled back the curtain covering one of the long windows to see sleet bouncing off the concrete as it hit the ground. It was ridiculous for ice to return the second week of April, but temperatures were expected to be above freezing later, so thankfully, this wouldn't last.

With a sigh, she dropped the curtain and resumed her trek to the office. Paperwork always accumulated over the weekend, and she might as well finish getting it caught up before the guests emerged from their rooms.

Huck quickened his noisy little steps as he tagged along. Tess had to admit—even if only to herself—that she was glad he had joined her this dismal morning.

Just as she and Huck stepped into the office, the front bell dinged. Frowning, she halted her steps, and they returned to the foyer. It was unusual for them to have guests this early, especially on such a foul-weathered morning.

An attractive, sixty-something-year-old African American man stood just inside the door, leaning heavily on a wooden cane. He looked a little unsure of himself, and his posture suggested he may be contemplating leaving. As his gaze fell on Tess, relief softened his worried expression. Beneath a groomed, nearly white mustache, his lips turned into a smile that reached his eyes. "Hello," he said. "Have I come at a bad time?"

Tess gave a dismissive wave of her hand and shook her head. "We officially open the doors at seven, but can I help you?" With a little yelp, Huck bounded around her and jumped up on the man. "I'm so sorry. Huck," she scolded. "Sit!"

The dog obeyed but stayed firmly planted at the man's feet.

"Friendly little guy, isn't he?"

"He usually doesn't act that way. Never, actually. What can I do for you?"

She couldn't recall there being a reservation for today. She'd double-checked the computer just before bed last night. Besides, check-in wasn't until afternoon.

The man hesitated just for a beat, then reached inside his coat pocket and pulled out a folded sheet of paper. "This may seem a little odd, but I think I had a reservation here in December."

"You *think* you had a reservation?" Tess walked forward and reached for the paper.

"I'm not sure, but as you can see, it appears that way."

Tess looked over pen scratches scrawling across the unlined paper. It had the name of the inn, a significant dollar amount that appeared to be equal to three months' lodging, and the date—December 1. She looked up and met his questioning gaze. How could someone not know if he'd made a reservation four months ago, paid an exorbitant amount of money, and then never shown up?

She smelled a scam and narrowed her eyes, yet something familiar about the information on the page started to seep into her memory, making her second-guess her knee-jerk suspicion.

"I should explain." The man nodded toward the paper in her hand. "On the first of December, I skidded on a patch of ice just outside of town and crashed my rental car. At least, that's what I've been told. I woke with no memories prior to the accident. And unfortunately, it's all still a blank."

Before Tess could form words or even a thought about what she'd just been told, movement from the corner of her eye caught her attention and caused her to turn. Janice Eastman held on to the wooden railing as she descended the long, open steps, a pleasant smile curving her lips. "Oh, we have a guest. Good morning." She reached out a hand to the visitor and widened her smile. "I'm Janice."

"Titus Jones." He shook her hand. "Nice to meet you. As I was just telling..." He frowned a little, glancing at Tess.

"Tess," she said. "Janice and I are business partners."

"And friends for forty years," Janice said in her cheery-even-before-coffee voice. Her matching personality had won the hearts of practically everyone who had ever met the platinum-blond-haired widowed minister's wife.

Tess handed Janice the paper. "Titus thinks he may have had a reservation in December. Why does that seem so familiar?"

Janice sucked in her bottom lip as she read, then suddenly glanced up at the man, eyes wide. She cast a glance at Tess, then back to the man.

"Tess, you remember." She looked at Titus. "You must be 'money-order man'!"

The man's eyebrows rose, but humor glinted in his eyes.

"Money-order man?" he said. "I'm not sure..."

"He doesn't remember making the reservation or paying for it," Tess said. "Apparently, he was in an accident on the way here that day and doesn't remember anything before it."

"That would explain a lot." Janice gave the man a reassuring smile. "You've been a mystery for months."

"I apologize..."

"Oh, don't apologize. If anyone loves a mystery, it's us. Right, Tess? Besides, you couldn't help it." She shook her head. "Amnesia...it's almost like a movie!"

"It does seem like a fiction plot." He frowned. "I suppose I would describe it more as a horror flick though," he said, his tone wistful.

"How insensitive of me." Janice touched his arm. "Tess, how can we figure out if Titus is the one who made those reservations?"

"I can look it up," Tess said. "What was the name on the reservation?"

"Titus Jones."

"You remember your name, but nothing else?"

"My identification was in my wallet," he said matter-of-factly.

"Oh, of course."

Janice shot Tess a frown that told her she was being less than gracious. And she probably was, which made her feel a twinge of guilt, especially after the sermon Sunday about being careful of how you treat strangers. She highly doubted Titus Jones was an angel sent by God, but the least she could do was check him out. "I'll see what I can find," she said, using a little more accommodating tone.

Janice lifted her gaze to the tall stranger. "The café hasn't officially opened yet, but as it just so happens, we know the owners. We can get you a cup of coffee. Or do you prefer tea? Or do you even remember which you prefer?"

He chuckled. "To be honest, I don't know how I felt about coffee before December, but I can say that I am more than a little fond of a good strong cup or two in the morning these days. And I prefer tea in the evening."

"Good! Come on. We can probably find something for breakfast too. On the house."

"Oh, no. I couldn't—"

Tess shook her head. Janice loved to "on the house" things. Of course, she and LuAnn had given away their share of coffee, pastries, and soup too.

Predictably, Janice didn't hear a word of his protest. "A good breakfast with a cup of coffee is a must on a morning like this. Can you believe it's still all wintry out there?"

Annoyance filled Tess as Huck followed after Janice. The little traitor. She remained where she was, watching them walk toward the café as their voices trailed. Janice stopped and looked back. "Coming, Tess?"

She nodded. "In just a minute. I need to stop by the office and check on that reservation."

They disappeared into the café, and Tess walked the few steps to the office. She had barely turned the key in the lock, settled into the chair, and set her coffee cup on the desk when Janice appeared at the door. Tess raised her eyebrows. "What did you do with Mr. Jones?"

"Winnie is fussing over him. He gave me this." She handed Tess a business card. "He thought it might help you confirm his story."

Tess glanced at the card.

"It's his psychiatrist," Janice said. "She's been working with him to recover memories since the medical doctors can't find a physical reason for his amnesia. I feel pretty sure he's our mystery man from December. And I have to say, you seem awfully suspicious. I think you're making him uncomfortable. Which isn't very nice."

"I'm just checking his reservation. If he's the same man, we'll give him back his money order, and he can be on his way."

"At least give the man the benefit of checking out his story before you suspect him of lying."

"I know. But you have to admit we've dealt with a lot of shady characters these past few months."

The frown lines between Janice's eyes softened. "I suppose you have a point. Still . . . Huck is really taken with him, and you know they say if a dog likes someone, then they must be a good person. Dogs can sense that kind of thing."

Affection for her soft-hearted friend surged in Tess's chest. She refrained from snarking back that a dog would follow anyone who gave him a smile and a scratch. "I'll look up the amount of the money order and confirm the date he was supposed to check in."

"What about the psychiatrist?"

Tess set the card on her desk next to her coffee cup, which seemed to be the safest place to set anything she didn't want to lose.

"It's a little early in the day to call a professional, don't you think?"

Janice grinned. "You'd have to *need* a professional to call one this early."

Tess returned the grin. "You'd better go check on our guest before Winnie forces him to eat a little of everything she's been cooking. You know food is her love language."

"I'm going." Janice hesitated. "You're coming though, right? LuAnn should be down soon."

"Ten minutes. Tops. I promise. Besides, LuAnn's already up."

Janice's eyebrows rose. "She is?"

"Huck was an early riser."

Janice chuckled as she walked away.

When she was once again alone in her office, Tess opened her file-folder drawer and found the envelope marked INVALID ADDRESS. When it became apparent that their guest would not be arriving, she had attempted to return the money order to the address she'd been given, only to have it come back a week later.

Tess had taken the reservation herself, and though she normally wouldn't have made it without a credit card, it had been far enough in advance that the man had time to back it up with the money order he sent. And she had been moved with compassion when he told her he had recently experienced the death of a loved one and wanted to get away from well-meaning friends and family to come to grips with her death. She assumed it was his wife he was talking about, and she could certainly understand his feelings. The reservation had come in just around the anniversary of her Jeffrey's death. She found the four-month-old file and confirmed that the information on the paper matched the computer records and the amount of the money order.

Her eye caught the card containing the number for Titus Jones's psychiatrist. She shrugged. There was really no point in calling, since the rest of the information checked out. But as she shut off the light and locked the office door, she couldn't shake the questions niggling her brain. Most of the information had checked out, but not all of it. Amnesia might explain their visitor not showing up on time, but it didn't explain why he had given them an invalid address four months ago.

CHAPTER TWO

Janice looked up as Tess entered the dining room. Winnie motioned to a seat across from Titus. "Give me that cup," she said. "I'll get you some fresh coffee and breakfast."

Grateful, Tess handed over her mug, which was still half full of cooled coffee. "Thank you, Winnie. But just the coffee, please. I'm not hungry."

Winnie huffed. It never boded well for any of them to turn down food and risk the wrath of Winnie.

As she took her seat, Tess held up the envelope and focused her attention on Titus. "I confirmed the reservation. I just need to see your identification in order to return your money."

After all, three months' worth of accommodation was a lot of money, and they certainly could not turn over a refund just on his word that he was an amnesiac who would very much like to have his money back.

"Of course." Seeming not at all offended by her request, he reached into his jacket pocket and withdrew his wallet. He shook his head as he handed over his driver's license. "I don't even know that man."

Janice touched his arm in apparent sympathy. "Have they given you any hope you'll recover your memories?"

A quick glance at the ID confirmed that the man was owed a refund. Tess slid the envelope across the table with a twinge of regret. Winter months were typically slow for businesses such as theirs. Though the inn hadn't done too poorly, she looked forward to what looked to be a promising spring and summer.

"I was unconscious for a few days." He took his license and stuffed it back into his wallet as he addressed Janice's question. "But according to the doctors, there doesn't seem to be a medical reason that I haven't gotten my memory back."

"That's got to be frustrating," Janice said.

He released a sigh. "It is. Sometimes it feels like the memories are almost there. Like when you walk into a room and forget why you went in the first place."

Winnie chuckled. "Happens to me all the time."

"You're not kidding," Janice piped in. "The older I get, the more of those senior moments I have."

Tess nodded toward his wallet as he returned it to his jacket pocket. "The address on your license doesn't exist, according to the post office. As you can see, we tried to return the money order to you."

He fingered the envelope. "That, I'm afraid, is another source of frustration, as you can imagine." His brow creased with a frown. "I do know from police records that I rented the car in New Jersey. But does that mean I'm from there? I investigated, tried to find a family member or friend who could shed some light on my life before December, but I came up empty."

"I imagine that's got to stick in your craw," Winnie said, setting a full, steaming mug in front of Tess, along with a plate laden with bacon, scrambled eggs, a blueberry muffin, and a few grapes. Winnie shrugged before turning her attention back to their guest. "It's frustrating enough when I can't remember something as simple as a name or an ingredient."

"Or that I said I wasn't hungry," Tess said, teasing, although she had to admit the smell of the food was tantalizing, and she could feel her appetite waking up.

Winnie gave her an offhanded wave. "You've got to eat."

Titus fixed an approving smile on Winnie. "After months of hospital and rehab food, this is heavenly."

The fastest way to Winnie's heart was to appreciate the fruits of her labor, and if a person threw in divine comparisons, so much the better. She practically beamed beneath the praise. "Your plate's about empty. I'll be right back." She rose before he could answer, and walked to the kitchen.

Janice, who had been silent for longer than was typical of her, took a deep breath and exhaled. "By 'rehab,' I assume you were transferred to a facility for physical therapy?"

He nodded. "I broke my right leg and right arm. They tell me I was thrown from the vehicle, and I was pinned beneath it when the paramedics arrived. It's been a process to gain enough mobility to walk at all, and then only with a cane."

"I take it you've been released from medical care?" Tess asked, wondering how on earth he could have paid for months of care and rehab without a credit card or access to any kind of account. But that wasn't her concern, so as difficult as it was, she forced herself not to ask such personal questions.

"I still need some physical therapy, but they've released me from the rehabilitation center." He glanced at the envelope and hesitated. "I wonder..."

"Yes?" Janice said, using her soft pastor's-wife tone to encourage him to continue.

"I've been staying temporarily at the apartment of one of the medical assistants from the facility. But I hate feeling like such an intrusion on him, and I'd like to find a place of my own." His gaze swept around the table, taking in the women. "Would you happen to have a room available?"

"I assume you're talking about an extended stay?" Tess wasn't sure she wanted a mystery man staying at the inn for a lengthy amount of time. What if he brought trouble with him?

He nodded. "Is that possible?"

"How long do you think you will need to stay?"

"My physical therapy team is encouraged with my progress," he said. "They think I'll be released from their care completely within the next two or three weeks. My psychiatrist hasn't even ventured a guess. She believes my memory could flip on like a switch—or never return. But if I could stay here until I'm released from physical therapy, I'd appreciate it."

Tess's mind went to the reservations she'd checked on the night before. All but one guest would be checking out today, so that left seven rooms available, not to mention the honeymoon suite, which wasn't occupied at the moment.

"Tess?" Janice interrupted her thoughts.

Tess nodded. "We do have vacancies. But if our current guests check out at the last minute as they tend to do, it'll probably be midafternoon before we have a room ready for you."

"That's fine. I'd be grateful." He slid the envelope back across the table to Tess. "Will this cover my stay?"

Tess hesitated, hating to cause an awkward moment. But it had to be said. "I'll have to check with the bank to confirm the validity of the money order."

"But I'm sure it'll be just fine," Janice said quickly.

"Of course," Titus said. He frowned. "It's odd that I didn't use a credit card to make my reservation. There were none in my wallet either."

If he truly didn't remember anything at all from his past, Tess hated to bring up the reason he had given her for coming here—so he could grieve his wife's passing in solitude and on his own terms. "Titus..." She hesitated only because she didn't want to be the source of his grief. But if this man was truly trying to recover his memories, the truth might help provide some answers. She would want that herself.

The room remained silent as the group around the table waited for her to continue. She gathered a breath and exhaled. "First of all. Yes, there is quite a bit more than a month of payment in that money order. You intended to stay for three months, so even paying for the month in advance, you have a refund coming."

His face softened with relief. "That's good news." His lips turned up into a wry grin. "Provided I wasn't a con artist and the money order turns out to be a fake."

Winnie returned carrying a basket of pastries and set them in front of Titus. "You're no con artist. I have a nose for these things." She nodded toward the basket. "Eat up."

"I shouldn't." He hesitated for only a millisecond, then chuckled, reaching into the basket. "But how can I resist?"

Winnie smiled. "Strawberry scones are always a good choice."

Tess hated to throw a wet blanket on the sudden levity, but she knew it wasn't fair to the man not to give him the rest of the information. "Titus," she said slowly, "there's more I should probably tell you."

"What is it, Tess?" Janice asked. Tess hadn't told her two friends about Titus's reason for needing privacy in a quiet town like Marietta. He had specifically asked that she not share any of his personal details with anyone and, with the holidays upon them, it had all just slipped her mind.

She caught Titus's gaze, and he leaned in, his expression somber and waiting. "If you know something else, I'd appreciate the information."

Tess continued, though it was difficult to meet his gaze, considering the news she had to give him. "I'm the one you spoke to when you made your reservation. I am also the one who made the decision to allow the booking without a credit card, which is against policy." She hesitated, then went on. "I'm sorry to tell you this, but at the time, you told me you wanted to remain anonymous, that you wanted to get away from well-meaning family and friends."

Confusion clouded his eyes. "That doesn't seem…"

Tess swallowed hard. "It would seem that you are a widower. You said you needed a quiet, peaceful place to mourn your recent loss."

All the strength seemed to leave his body, and he slumped back in his chair, staring at the half-eaten strawberry scone on his plate. They gave him his moment, respecting the silence. Finally, he raised his head. "That would explain the sense of loss I've felt. My psychiatrist believed it was just because I lost my memories, but I've felt as though it is something more. Did I tell you my late wife's name or ..." He shifted his eyes until he focused directly on Tess. "Did I mention children ... or grandchildren?"

Tess shook her head. "I'm so sorry, you only said family and friends. So who those family members might be, I couldn't say. And you didn't give me her name. I wish I had pressed for more information."

"No, please don't feel bad. This is more information than I've had in months. I'm grateful to know anything at all."

The door opened and LuAnn breezed in, dressed for the day. She headed straight for the coffeepot. "Good morning," she said. She poured her coffee, her back to them. She turned and took a sip as she walked, then her eyes fell on Titus. Looking at each of them in turn, she clearly noted the somber mood and frowned. "What'd I miss?"

⚬━━━━━⚬❀⚬━━━━━⚬

Two hours passed quickly as the café filled up for breakfast and turned over several times. As their weekend guests slowly began to make their way from their rooms to check out, Tess found she had no time to make the call to Western Union to verify the money order. Janice's voice carried from the foyer as she walked the last couple to the door just before noon.

Robin, their occasional all-around go-to gal, waved and flashed her dimples as she muscled the cleaning cart to the elevator. "Wish me luck!" she called. Tess chuckled. Cleaning all the rooms in a few hours could be a challenge, especially when everyone checked out around the same time.

"You've got this," Tess said with a reassuring smile.

When the elevator doors closed, Tess turned her attention back to the screen in front of her and checked the reservations page again. Besides Titus, two more rooms had been booked online, and guests would be arriving by three. She noted one of the couples had booked the honeymoon suite for the rest of the week. She sighed when she recognized the name on the reservation: Karl Mannus. The news anchor at Channel 8 had done no less than three stories about the inn over the past few months. Surely he hadn't come to do another. They did appreciate the publicity, but Tess had been hoping to convince the station to pick up the community Easter egg hunt they were planning.

LuAnn joined her at the check-in desk. "Goodness, the café is hopping today. And you know the Bickerton ladies are coming in for lunch." She grinned. "They made a reservation. How cute is that?" She peered closer at Tess. "What's that look about?"

Tess pointed at the computer screen. "Did you know Karl Mannus booked the honeymoon suite all week?"

A hint of humor lit LuAnn's eyes. "For him and his ego? Or is he bringing a bride?"

Tess chuckled. "There's a note here that says it's his tenth anniversary."

LuAnn's eyebrows went up. "Hmm, maybe he's a deeper well than we gave him credit for."

Tess shrugged, still staring at the page. "Maybe. Robin must have taken the reservation."

"At least the honeymoon suite is booked," LuAnn said. "And it's kind of sweet, don't you think?"

"What's sweet?" Janice said, joining them.

"Karl Mannus and his wife booked the honeymoon suite for the week. It's their tenth anniversary."

Janice blinked in surprise. "I didn't even know he was married. I hope he's not planning another story about us while he's here though. I'm still getting calls about the antiques he put on the news after he promised he wouldn't."

LuAnn laughed and slipped her arm around Janice's shoulders. "Remember, this too shall pass."

Tess turned to Janice. "What did you do with Titus?"

With a quick palm to her cheek, Janice glanced toward the sitting room. "Goodness, gracious goat. I forgot all about the poor man."

"No worries," LuAnn said. "He left not too long ago to pick up his things from the apartment where he's been staying."

The bell above the front door dinged, and the three of them turned to see who had arrived.

"Karl Mannus," Janice said, under her breath.

22

The news anchor walked in, carrying two bags. A red-headed woman walked next to him, looking around as she took everything in. Tess liked her immediately. As the couple approached the counter, the woman caught Tess staring and offered a shy, warm smile that scrunched the freckles on her nose and sprang to her very-blue eyes. "Hey, ladies," Karl said, as if he considered them old friends.

"Karl," Janice said around a smile. "You're early for check-in."

"Is that okay?" He set the bags on the floor in front of the counter. "The lady on the phone said the suite would be ready any time after eleven."

LuAnn smiled at him. "Robin would be the one to know if it's ready. I'll just call up there and make sure."

She hung up a minute later. "Let's get you checked in, and you're all set. Are you going to introduce us to your wife, Karl?"

His cheeks darkened. "I'm sorry." He put his arm around his wife and pulled her closer to him. "Honey, these are the owners of the inn."

Tess smiled. "I'm Tess, this is Janice, and LuAnn."

Karl's wife smiled. "I'm Shyla. I've been wanting to visit the inn ever since I heard you were restoring it." Her eyes shone as she glanced around and waved a slender hand, sweeping the room. "It's just beautiful."

"It's true. She's been talking about coming here for months." Karl tightened his grip on Shyla's shoulder. "We thought our anniversary was a good excuse."

Janice smiled in a way that reached her eyes. "Ten years is a milestone." Clearly, she was as taken by Karl's tenderness with his wife as Tess was. "It's good you could take the time off, Karl."

"It doesn't happen very often, that's for sure." He glanced toward the café. "We thought we'd get a bite to eat and then scope out Mrs. O'Hara's house."

LuAnn gave a nod of approval. "It's one of the best landmarks in Marietta. They give tours during certain months. But with Mrs. O'Hara's birthday party on Friday, I doubt there'll be a tour this week."

Shyla grinned as she met LuAnn's gaze. "Karl is covering the party, so we'll get to go inside. Will you ladies be there?"

"We will!" Janice's excitement was clear in her tone. "It's such a beautiful home. And it's the party of the year here in Marietta. Winnie, that's our cook—"

"And dear friend," LuAnn broke in.

"Of course she's our friend, but goodness, we'd be out of our depth if we hadn't hired her." She turned her gaze back to Shyla. "Anyway, Winnie, our cook *and* dear friend, is catering the event."

"I'll be working, so I won't have much time to eat while I'm there." Karl tucked the room keys inside his coat pocket and reached for his bags.

"It's nice that you're covering Mrs. O'Hara's birthday," Tess said, forcing herself not to be shocked that Karl was mixing work with a romantic trip for his wife. After all, if Shyla didn't seem to mind, what was it to Tess?

He gave them a conspiratorial grin, showing off his bright white teeth. "That's the official reason. But"—his eyes took on a hint of excitement—"rumor has it, the old lady has family ties to the mafia. That's what I'm hoping to uncover. Did you know her sister is one of the Kellys of New York? As in the mob family? Or she was until she passed away last year. That's how I found out about the connection. When I did an internet search for Molly O'Hara, Mrs. Kelly's obituary mentioned that she was survived by a son and daughter-in-law and one sister: Molly O'Hara of Marietta, Ohio."

"I had no idea," Tess said, nor had she ever heard of the Kelly family he was talking about. But maybe, of all the people who had tried to dig up a story about the O'Haras, Karl had the tenacity to actually make it happen.

"I just need to connect the O'Haras to the Kellys' criminal activities."

Tess listened with mixed feelings. Who was to say that one side of the family had to be involved in the nefarious doings of the other side of the family? And with Molly's son and grandson both in law enforcement and her great-grandson, Justin, a firefighter, the O'Haras seemed more like heroes than villains.

Shyla pressed a palm to Karl's bicep. "If there's anything to uncover, sweetheart, you'll find it."

The sudden tenderness in his eyes revealed that Karl Mannus loved more than just his career.

Part of Tess hoped Karl would uncover a little mischief around Molly O'Hara's husband. They'd all heard the mob rumors for years, but to Tess's knowledge, there'd never been one shred of proof to tie the O'Hara family to a crime syndicate. She winked at Shyla and said, "Here's to finding a smoking gun."

"Thank you. Now, which way to the honeymoon suite?"

LuAnn pointed toward the stairs. "It's on the next floor. Or you can take the elevator."

The couple exchanged a glance and said at the same time, "Stairs."

"You just never know about a person, do you?" Janice said after Karl and Shyla had walked away.

LuAnn pursed her lips. "I've never really considered there might be a relaxed, man-in-love side to Karl."

Janice leaned against the counter. "He's either crazy about his wife or he's the best actor I've ever seen."

Tess couldn't resist a chuckle. "Better than Humphrey Bogart?"

Janice grinned. "Is anyone better than Bogie?"

LuAnn tilted her head and glanced up as the bell above the door rang in the foyer. She lowered her tone a bit. "Do you think he'll find something that proves the O'Haras have mob connections?"

Janice shrugged. "Every few years, for as far back as I can remember, the rumors start circulating again, but no one has ever found anything concrete that I know of."

"Oh well, if there's anything to find out, my guess is Karl's the man for the job," Tess said.

"And if not, it'll be fun watching him chase his tail a little." Janice winked.

Tess chuckled. She couldn't help but agree, but as Titus walked toward them, carrying a duffel bag and leaning heavily on his cane, the thought occurred to her that they had a mystery of their own on their hands.

CHAPTER THREE

The Bickerton sisters were as spunky as any little old ladies alive who had lived nearly a century. There was nothing fragile about their minds, though their bodies were frailer than either wanted to admit.

Before coming to work at the inn, Winnie had worked for the sisters, and she still cooked for them every now and then. But apparently, Thelma had a taste for Winnie's creamy corn chowder, so she had braved the cold, damp day to get a bowl.

Tess rarely missed a chance to have a conversation with either of the Bickerton sisters, although Irene was technically a Martin by marriage.

A knock on her door told her that Brad Grimes had arrived with his aunts. At her beckoning, Taylor peeked in. "They're asking for you."

"I'm coming."

The café lunch crowd had all but gone by the time she greeted her friends around the six-seated table. Except for Shyla Mannus, who sat alone at a table next to theirs, there were no other diners. LuAnn and Brad sat next to each other, and the two sisters sat at the ends. That left the other two seats for Janice and Tess. Janice smiled and patted the table in front of the empty chair next to her.

Tess waved at Shyla, who had just looked up from a book. "Would you like to join us?"

She smiled. "Karl's making some calls. He'll be here soon. But thank you."

Janice leaned over. "She's been sitting there a while. I hope Karl's not standing her up."

Tess would have loved to insist Shyla join them, but before she could extend the offer again, Taylor set a bowl of soup in front of her. And Shyla returned to her book.

Over large bowls of chowder and baskets of crispy french bread, the conversation inevitably turned to Molly O'Hara's birthday party.

"Will you be there Friday, ladies?" Tess asked.

"To be sure," Irene said, patting her chin with a napkin. "We haven't seen Molly in quite some time."

"Not since she started losing her marbles," Thelma added. "Last time we had tea in her garden, she told us she'd have us whacked if we didn't stop flirting with her husband."

Irene snorted. "Her husband was a fat, red-faced, drunken fool with an eye for the ladies, that's for sure. But we certainly never flirted with him. Besides, he's been dead for thirty-five years. They say the brakes on his car failed, but if you want my opinion, he was the one who got himself whacked."

LuAnn laughed. "Whacked?"

"Oh, sure. You know Mr. O'Hara was a mobster from way back. When their son joined the police force he almost disowned him."

"So you honestly think there's a connection between the O'Haras and organized crime?" Could it be that Karl was truly onto something, and the ladies were right about the O'Haras? Maybe he would find what others had tried and failed to uncover over the years.

"Have you been living under a rock?" The look on Thelma's face was a clear indication she thought Tess wasn't firing on all cylinders.

Heat rose to Tess's cheeks. "We thought those were just rumors. I'm pretty sure everyone in town thinks the same thing."

Except Karl Mannus. At the thought of Karl, Tess's gaze shifted to Shyla, who had abandoned her book and was trying to surreptitiously listen in on the conversation. Tess motioned her over. Shyla smiled shyly and shook her head.

"How long have the O'Haras lived in Marietta?"

Tess addressed the question to either of the older ladies. Irene turned immediately to her sister. "Do you remember?"

"The family is almost as old in this town as the Bickertons."

Tess couldn't help but smile. Had Thelma forgotten that Howard Bickerton had been responsible for building the inn before the Civil War? Of course, they had discovered he had been killed before he could disembark in Marietta, but it was his vision that had built the very building they were currently sitting in. "I was under the impression that the first time the O'Haras came to Marietta was when Molly was a young bride, in the early forties."

Thelma nodded. "Yes. That monstrosity they call a house was her wedding present."

LuAnn exchanged a look with Tess, then Janice, but they hid their confusion from the ladies.

"The first Mr. O'Hara lived here during the war though. I'm not sure if he fought in it or not." Thelma turned to her sister. "Do you remember?"

"I don't. I'd forgotten all about him."

Again, Tess exchanged glances with her friends. Brad was the one who spoke up. "Do you mean World War II?"

Thelma shook her head. "No, of course not. The O'Haras and Kellys didn't fight in that war. By then they were able to buy their way out of the draft." She included each person at the table in a queenly scan. "When they were all young, they'd visit back and forth between New York and here." She gave a dreamy sigh. "Frank Sinatra even made an appearance at a couple of the O'Hara parties here in Marietta. What a time that was." Her eyes took on a faraway look, and it seemed as though she had checked in to days gone by and forgotten about the conversation. But suddenly she perked back up and returned to the present with a gleam in her sharp eyes. "Make no mistake. Now that Figgy Kelly in New York has passed, and Molly O'Hara is going downhill fast, there's a scramble for who will take over the two families."

"What are you saying, Thelma?" Janice asked. "Who is Figgy Kelly?"

Irene cleared her throat loudly, drawing everyone's attention, but her narrowed gaze was firmly fixed on her sister.

Thelma released a heavy breath. "If you have something to say, Irene, just say it."

"And get myself whacked?"

Apparently, *whacked* was the word of the day with the sisters. But Irene's anxiety over the information her sister seemed free to share was real.

"Don't be ridiculous. Who's going to bother with an old lady? Besides, all of the really dangerous men are long gone. The young O'Hara boys are squeaky clean and there to protect us, and there's only one Kelly boy left in New York, and he's in his fifties." Thelma's lips twisted a little. "And from what I hear, he's nothing like his father and his grandfather. And I don't mean that in a flattering way for the younger Kelly." She cocked her head toward Janice. "Figgy is Molly O'Hara's sister. She was married to Nolan Kelly, the head of the Kelly family in New York. He was an awful fellow. She passed away a few months ago, just before the holidays, so Molly is the last of that group."

Janice gave Tess and then LuAnn a wide-eyed look. Figgy Kelly's obituary was the one that Karl had used to discover the tie between the two families. Maybe there was more to the O'Hara mob connection than anyone had ever truly believed. LuAnn shrugged, clearly thinking similar thoughts.

Tess realized they'd gotten completely off the original topic. "Thelma, if you weren't talking about World War II, what did you mean about the first Mr. O'Hara living in Marietta during the War?"

Thelma blinked, then her eyebrows went up. "Oh, yes. We did go off on a rabbit trail, didn't we?" She chuckled. "Haven't you read the diary, dear?"

LuAnn leaned forward. They had all read parts of Prudence Willard's journal, but LuAnn had devoured it. "Do you mean Prudence's diary?"

"Of course. She wrote about Jack."

LuAnn frowned and looked from Tess to Janice. "I'll have to look again. If she just used the name 'Jack,' I wouldn't have connected it to the O'Haras."

"Then I suggest you do go look again." Thelma dipped her spoon into her chowder. "Right, Irene?"

"But does that mean the O'Haras left Marietta after the Civil War? Why would they leave, and why would they return?"

"I can't remember." Thelma waved a thin hand. "But it's all in the diary."

Tess glanced at LuAnn, who shook her head again. How on earth could the sisters be so certain? They had always been sharp as tacks, and it was doubtful they would share the same faulty memory.

What did seem likely was that the Inn Crowd had just found themselves in the middle of yet another mystery.

Tess watched the clock and turned the lock on the front door at exactly eleven. Her packed-out day had started much too early, and she felt weary to the bone.

As she headed toward the stairs, she noticed someone had left the lamps on in the sitting room, which wasn't completely out of the ordinary. She walked toward the room to shut off all but the lamp next to the sofa, and found Titus Jones seated in a chair with a book in his lap.

"Titus. I thought everyone had gone to bed." Huck was curled up on the ottoman at his feet, snoozing contentedly. "Is he bothering you? I can take him upstairs. He usually sleeps in LuAnn's room."

Titus smiled and glanced at the dog. "When he came back in from his walk an hour or so ago, he seemed to want to stay. I promised LuAnn I'd take him upstairs with me. She mentioned you were working late in the office."

"I'm just about ready to head that way. I can take him."

"He's a nice little companion."

"Is there anything wrong with your room?" There was a nice leather chair and ottoman in Woodsmoke and Pine. He could have just as comfortably read his book in private.

His eyebrows went up. "No, of course not. It's the best room I can remember ever having." He chuckled at his own little joke. "I'm drawn to this room, for some reason. The bookshelves and grand piano, everything feels, I don't know, familiar to me. I thought if I stayed in here long enough, some…memory might present itself."

Had he left a cozy home with books and music and family? Tess realized she'd never gotten around to calling Western Union to verify the money order. She couldn't imagine the man sitting here being some kind of scam artist. She usually had good instincts about people. Her years as a teacher had honed her senses to recognize a lie when she heard it. But while she didn't necessarily believe Titus had lied about any of the information he'd shared, she couldn't help but wonder if he'd withheld some of the truth. For instance, why were there no credit cards in his name? He'd brought up the question himself at breakfast. Was he genuinely curious or just trying to throw them off the scent? And why did his New Jersey address not exist, according to the postal service? She set the thoughts aside when he reached out and lifted Huck.

"I suppose it's getting late." He suppressed a yawn as he set the dog on the floor. Huck stretched and yawned, then gave a little yelp and dipped his head toward his hind leg.

"What's the matter, Huck?" Tess stooped down and discovered the source of his distress. "Poor little guy. His nail got caught on the throw rug." She loosened his nail carefully and gathered him into her arms. "I'm so sorry." She tossed a glance at Titus, who reached out and scratched Huck behind the ears. Tess sighed. "I guess I better call the groomer in the morning to get those nails clipped." The situation had gone beyond annoyance at clicking nails on the floor. They couldn't have Huck hurt because they were too busy. One of them would just have to take a little time off to tend their dog.

Keeping Huck tucked in close against her chest, Tess headed to the door. Titus followed. Stepping aside, Tess allowed him to precede her from the room. She turned off the overhead light, leaving a small lamp glowing in case any of their other guests came down during the night for a book.

As they walked toward the steps, Tess hesitated. "Would you prefer the elevator?"

He shook his head. "The exercise helps strengthen my muscles."

The hard lines of concentration on his face showed that the effort was painful. Tess's heart went out to him, and she admired his determination. She wondered if there were times that he concentrated as hard on trying to recover his memory as he did his physical recovery.

He glanced up, and his eyes questioned her. "Is everything okay, Tess?"

Her face warmed under his scrutiny. "I was just thinking about how difficult it must be trying to remember a lifetime. I have to admit I was just being curious. I'm sorry."

"Don't be. It's a curious condition. You can ask anything."

She hesitated a second, not wanting to impose. But he had said to ask, and maybe it helped not having everyone avoid talking about the condition. "Do you ever have flashes of memory or mind pictures, dreams, anything at all?"

"Sadly, no. Not even..." He expelled a sigh. "Not even the wife you mentioned. If we had a family, they must be panicking about my absence. Unless..." His eyes clouded with a pain that no one could have faked unless they were Cary Grant. "I find myself wondering if maybe I'm a bad father, or not close to my kids, if I have any. Surely, in today's technological world, a grown child would have the tools to find his or her father. Wouldn't you think?"

Tess's heart softened. He had a good point. But then again... "Titus, didn't you say that the police and your medical team have all been trying to discover your identity for months? If they couldn't find anything, how could someone armed only with an internet search engine?"

He nodded, his expression still dark. "After all these months, I've figured out that I must have changed my identity. Otherwise, my name should have pulled up some information. Wouldn't you think?"

"That's a possibility."

"What sort of man is so selfish he would deny his family the ability to find him for four months? If I wasn't a horrible man, they must feel so abandoned."

"But how could you have possibly known you would have the accident? I'm sure you would have contacted any family to let them know you were fine."

He stopped and turned to her and patted her arm. "You're a kind woman, Tess. I appreciate the benefit of the doubt. I only hope I deserve your faith in me."

Tess watched as he held tightly to the railing and climbed the steps. She wished he had used the elevator rather than taking the stairs, exercise or no. But sometimes a man had to choose the difficult path to feel better about things. Or perhaps Titus was taking the difficult path as a way of punishing himself for his perceived shortcomings. One thing was clear, he was battling even the idea that he had once hurt those he loved.

Tess couldn't help but imagine how terrible it must be to find out you had a spouse who had passed away and not remember one day of the life and love you shared. As much as she still missed Jeffrey, at least he was alive in every memory, photograph, and video.

April 6, 1863

Prudence stepped forward, only to be yanked back by Jason's strong hand wrapped around her arm. "Does thee want that dog to tear Moses apart?" Jason's low warning tone broke through the icy fear, and common sense returned. He was right. Any act of aggression would make the animal attack. Prudence had seen, firsthand, the damage a bloodhound could do if provoked.

"Moses, sweetheart," she said, her throat trembling with her words. "I want thee to stay very still. Mama and Papa are here." She turned to Jason. "What is thee going to do?" she whispered. Her eyes shifted to a long hoe in his hand. It wasn't much, but she was grateful he'd had the foresight to snatch it up from the garden spot. Without comment, he limped a step forward, keeping his gaze fixed on the growling canine. Jason continued a slow forward motion until he had closed by half the gap between him and their son. The dog growled, his full attention focused on Jason now.

"Pru," Jason said softly. "Go into the house and bring out that ham thee was going to bake for tomorrow's dinner."

Prudence gasped at the thought of giving the last ham from their smokehouse to that animal. But to save her son, she had no choice.

"There is a child lying in the grass just beyond Moses. I do not know if he is dead or only unconscious. Either way, I can only assume the dog is protecting him. Back up slowly toward the house. And bring my shotgun just in case I have no choice. Now, go."

Prudence did as she was bidden, but as she looked at the ham that was to have been their dinner the next day, she quickly snatched a butcher knife from the counter and hacked off a chunk large enough to keep the animal occupied without surrendering their entire meal. She held it close and grabbed the gun from its hiding place, praying she wouldn't have to use it. The last thing she wanted to do was harm an animal that was only protecting a child.

She found Jason and Moses exactly as she'd left them, her son, frozen in fear, Jason speaking in low, reassuring tones. The breeze caught the smoky scent of the ham, and the dog sniffed the air. With great caution, Prudence crept forward. It seemed an eternity before she reached Jason.

"Give me the ham, Wife. Have the gun ready."

Shaking her head, Prudence pressed the length of the gun against him until he took it. "Thee is a better shot. I will deal with the dog."

He heaved a frustrated sigh. She knew he didn't want both his wife and child in harm's way, but he didn't protest the truth of her words.

"Go slowly, now," he said. "Thee mustn't startle him."

Too frightened for her son, Prudence couldn't even muster the irritation she often felt when Jason spoke to her as though she were a child. Not when their own child and another were in danger. As she drew closer, it was all she could do not to toss the ham and draw Moses into her arms and make a run for it. But she couldn't risk the other child.

The dog took a menacing step forward as Prudence reached Moses.

"Mama? I'm scared."

"It is okay, Son," she said. "It is almost over. Just be very still. Thee is being a very big boy."

"Pru," Jason said. "Take two steps away from Moses. I don't have a clear shot."

Prudence stopped short of obeying as the child in the grass began to stir. A moan diverted the dog's attention. Relief flooded over Prudence as the child, whom she could now see was a boy, reached up and touched the animal. Clearly devoted to his young master, the dog sat and lowered his head, nuzzling the boy with a little whine.

"Pru?" Jason's tone held more insistence. Apparently, he had not seen what had just transpired.

"The child is rousing, Husband." With a shaky breath, Prudence knew this might be her best opportunity to get Moses out of harm's way. "Can thee be a very brave and obedient boy?" she whispered.

"Yes, ma'am."

"Very slowly, start walking backward toward thy papa. Can thee do that?"

"Yes," he whispered.

"When I count to three, start backing up. One...two... three..."

He obeyed, moving with excruciating slowness. The movement kept the dog on alert, but he kept his vigil over the conscious boy in the grass.

"Prudence, thee must get to the boy. Throw the ham, and the dog will go after it."

Gathering in a deep breath, Prudence prayed as she tossed the chunk of ham a few feet away from the child. The dog turned his head and sniffed the air again, but amazingly, he stayed put.

"Jason?"

"Boy!" Jason called. "Is thee awake? My wife and I are trying to help thee, but the dog will not allow us to get close to thee. I do not want to shoot him."

The grass moved as the child sat up slowly. Prudence caught her breath. He was small, but clearly a few years older than Moses. His arms were rail thin. Holding on to the dog for support, he stood shakily.

The dog whined as the boy walked on unsteady legs toward the ham. He was so thin, Prudence caught her breath. He motioned the bloodhound toward the ham, and the dog attacked the food with a ferocity that made Prudence shudder, though she knew his vigor was borne of hunger.

She silently motioned to the child, and he moved toward her. The dog raised his head and started to follow, but the boy stopped him with a palm-down motion that seemed to soothe him.

Prudence breathed a sigh when the child reached her. "Where has thee come from?" she asked.

He acknowledged her with wide brown eyes. His clothing was filthy and tattered and his hair matted. It was clear he was a runaway. But how far he'd come, she couldn't even fathom. One thing she was sure of. This child had found his way to their home by the hand of God and no other.

CHAPTER FOUR

Tess glanced in the rearview mirror as Huck whined and barked and whined again from his puppy carrier in the back seat. He seemed almost panicked. "It's okay, boy," she soothed. "We won't be in the car for long."

She'd made the call to their groomer and, as luck would have it, was able to get an appointment right away. With the memory of his nail painfully caught in the rug the night before, she ordered the spa package: wash, dry, nails, and all the other things groomers did to pamper animals. She hadn't planned on being the one to take him, but Janice's daughter, Stacy, had called at six thirty that morning with an emergency request. Larry was too sick for school, and Stacy needed an emergency babysitter while she went to take a test for college. She wouldn't be back before ten thirty or eleven. LuAnn had a meeting with their event planner about the Easter egg hunt—which they were calling Easter EGGstravaganza. That left Tess and Huck to go it alone. And he clearly wasn't a happy camper to be riding in the carrier. Not that she blamed the little guy. They'd pretty much given him the run of the inn as long as he didn't go into the food prep area or annoy the guests. He hadn't been confined except at night when they went upstairs to their suites on the fourth floor, and even then, he roamed the rooms. But judging by his reaction to the carrier—or maybe just being in the car—he seemed to be excessively distressed.

Tess continued her efforts, ineffectively, to soothe him with soft words for the next ten minutes until she pulled into a space in front of Sal's Bathe & Groom.

A smiling middle-aged woman wearing a scrubs top with paw prints all over it met them at the door introducing herself as Sally, owner of the shop. Sally offered Tess a pleasant enough greeting, then turned her attention to Huck. "Aren't you just a precious little guy!" Then her eyes clouded in concern. "Oh, poor thing. You're shaking like a leaf."

Tess set the carrier on the counter. "He wasn't too happy about being confined. I've never seen him so upset." She opened the door, and Huck practically hurled his little body into her arms. "Shh. It's okay." Tess held him close and stroked him until the shaking subsided.

"I remember this little guy," Sally said. "Brad Grimes brought him in a few months ago. He was a stray, wasn't he?"

"Yes, he was." Tess was gratified that Sally remembered Huck. She thought that was a good sign of how much the store owner cared about the animals she served.

"That might explain his aversion to cars," Sally said. "We don't know what kind of experiences he might have had before you found him. His previous owner could have dumped him on the side of a busy road, or he could even have been hit by a car." She smiled at Tess. "We'll just make sure he gets some extra TLC while he's here so hopefully he'll start to associate being in the car with good things."

Once Huck felt sufficiently brave enough to raise his head and take in his surroundings, Sally offered her hand for him to sniff, and he wagged his tail.

For the first time since walking inside, Tess looked around the store. She looked back at the owner. "There are no cages."

"Only for reptiles, rodents, and birds. And those are in a different room." Sally scooped Huck from Tess's arms. "Otherwise, we keep the dogs and cats in playpens. We don't like cages around here." She nuzzled Huck. "No, we don't. Cages are for bad guys, and you are a good, good boy, aren't you?"

The way Huck was eating up the woman's affection gave Tess a sense of peace about allowing him out of her sight while he got his bath and grooming. "Do you have a waiting room, or should I come back to get him?"

"Oh, come back this afternoon. There are a few appointments ahead of him."

Tess's eyebrows rose. "Oh? Am I early for his appointment? I could've sworn you said nine o'clock."

Sally took the leash Tess handed her. "I did. We typically have our dog mommies and daddies drop their fur babies off first thing, and we take them as they come in. Don't worry, Huck will have lots of friends to play with while he waits his turn."

Tess hesitated, hating to leave him. But what choice did she have? "Well then. I have some errands to run. And I suppose I can go eat lunch, then swing back by to get him. Do you think he'll be ready by twelve thirty or..." Not wanting to seem pushy, Tess left the question dangling.

"Probably." Sally offered a smile of understanding. "Don't worry. He'll be just fine." She held Huck in one arm and pulled a card from a container on the counter. "My cell phone number and the shop number are on this. And there's a link for a live streaming we have set up for nervous mommies to check on how their babies are doing."

"Oh, I'm not a nervous..."

With a comforting—and maybe a little patronizing—pat, Sally pressed the card into Tess's hand. Tess gave Huck a final scratch behind the ears, then rubbed his head. He rewarded her with a lick on her hand.

Back in her car, she turned the key. The engine kicked and whirred but didn't turn over. Dread twisted her stomach. "Not now." After a quick prayer and three more tries, the engine finally fired.

Letting the car idle, she pulled her cell phone from her purse and started to press her son's name but decided against it. She knew Jeff Jr. would likely fuss at her for spending money on a mechanic instead of letting him take a look at the car. She smiled, thinking of her boy. His father had taught him the way around a car, and the two of them had completely restored the 1953 Chevy pickup her son still drove. If anyone could figure out why her car was being testy about starting, it was Jeff Jr. But Tess was hesitant to add more to his already busy life. Instead, she googled the number for Ed Baxter, owner of Hilltop Auto Wrecking. He didn't just wreck non-running vehicles. He was an ace mechanic himself.

He answered on the fifth ring. "Hilltop Auto." He sounded breathless, as though he'd made a run for the phone. Tess inwardly cringed. He must be busy.

"Ed, this is Tess Wallace. I'm sorry to bother you."

"Hey, Tess. You're never a bother. What can I do for you?"

She told him what the car had done when she tried to start it.

"Sounds like the starter. You say it's running now?"

"Yes. Finally."

"Come on by, and I'll take a look at it."

"Are you sure you have time? I wouldn't want to impose."

"I always have time for you." He paused, then continued. "I won't take no for an answer. Come on by while the car is running. Be careful not to turn it off until you get here, or you might not get it going again."

His chivalrous attitude made Tess smile. She thanked him, promised to be there in just a few minutes, and disconnected the call. Before pulling away, she called LuAnn so that her friends didn't worry when she was gone for a few hours, rather than the hour she had expected.

"Do you need me to meet you at Ed's?" LuAnn asked. "In case he needs to keep your car for a day or two?"

"What about your meeting?"

"Oh, Kay had to push the meeting until this afternoon when her husband can get away from work. Apparently, her daughter is in the same class as Larry. Poor little thing has the same flu."

The smell of engine oil and cigarette smoke wafted through Ed's shop as he walked in from the garage area into the connecting customer area. "It's what I thought it was. Your starter's shot. It'll take a couple days to get a new one here. Just say the word, and I'll make the order right now."

Tess withheld a sigh. She'd been holding out hope that the car's problem was as simple as a belt or a loose wire. Something easy and quick that Ed could just fix while she waited for Huck's appointment to be finished. She looked at LuAnn, who sat on a ripped vinyl seat along the wall, sipping a cup of complimentary coffee.

"All right. Please order the part."

"Hang tight a minute, and I'll have an estimate for you."

She set her purse on the counter and reached for her wallet, but Ed had already picked up the cordless landline phone and pressed a button. He noted her purse and gave her a wave, shaking his head.

"Hey, Blue," he said, raising his voice as though the person on the other line was hard of hearing. He turned to Tess and lifted a "hang on a sec" index finger, then stepped through another door—presumably, his private office.

Ed's voice carried through the thin walls as he shot the breeze with Blue. Ten minutes later, Tess and LuAnn were still waiting as the door to the parking lot opened. One of Ed's employees entered carrying a small black duffel bag under his arm. Tess recognized him as one of the young adults who attended Christ Fellowship. His name tag said *Dane.* "Hi, Ms. Wallace, Ms. Sherill. You know where Ed is?"

He set the bag down against a free wall and waited impatiently for his boss. A scowl twisted his face as he heaved a frustrated breath. "There's no telling how long Ed'll be on the phone. Can you let him know this was pinned between the door and the seat of that Civic? He needs to call the police to tell the guy to come get it."

"Police?" LuAnn asked.

Dane nodded. "We've had that car out there for months. It was in an accident, and the rental company has finally released it for salvage. The old guy who was driving was hurt pretty bad. There were a couple of suitcases we sent to him right after the accident, but we missed this one somehow."

"I see," LuAnn said in a tone that Tess recognized as her "fishing for information" voice. "And the owner...?"

Dane shrugged. "He's been in the hospital, or rehab or something, from what I understand. I heard he has amnesia or something."

Clearly, he was talking about Titus. Or it was a dickens of a coincidence. "That poor man," LuAnn mumbled.

"Yeah. Well, not exactly *poor*, but it's got to be awful to lose your memory like that."

Tess and LuAnn exchanged a look. What did Dane know that they didn't? "What do you mean, he's 'not exactly poor'?"

A knowing grin stretched one side of Dane's mouth upward. He hesitated, casting a quick glance toward Ed's office, then leaned toward where they sat in the battered seats. "I'm not sure I should say anything."

Tess's heart rate picked up speed. Would he or wouldn't he spill the beans? Too bad Janice wasn't with them. She had taught many young people in Sunday school during the more than thirty years her husband had pastored Christ Fellowship. Tess recognized Dane from services, so there was a good chance he had been one of Janice's little sheep. She'd have been able to drag anything out of him.

LuAnn edged forward in her seat. "We have someone staying at the inn who might be the man you're describing." She turned to Tess. "The poor man mentioned an accident that left him with amnesia."

Tess nodded. "I hope whatever was in those suitcases isn't going to put our guests in danger." The thought had just crossed her mind, and now she envisioned a sniper rifle.

"Oh, don't worry. It's not dangerous. The police would be carting that off if it was anything like that." He pointed at the bag. "Just to put your mind at ease, I'll tell you. One of those suitcases was stuffed with piles of money." He shook his head. "If I were that rich, I'd rent an Audi or a Benz or something. Not a five-year-old Honda."

It just so happened the car Tess had brought in for him to fix was a five-year-old Honda. But he had a point. If she had a suitcase full of cash, she'd be driving something a little newer with some bells and whistles—like seat warmers.

But she didn't dwell on the thought as LuAnn pressed. "What do you mean, 'piles of money'?"

"Stacks of cash." He shrugged. "A lesser man might have had some sticky fingers. If the guy that owns it doesn't even remember he had it, he wouldn't notice if a little was missing."

He was rationalizing a bit too much for Tess's comfort. If they looked under his mattress would they find a stack or two of stolen bills? "Well…"

"Oh, don't worry." He grinned, his eyes flashing. "I said a lesser man. I've been getting things right with God for a while now. 'Thou shalt not steal,' you know."

Tess chuckled. "Good."

He backed toward the door. "You'll let Ed know to call the police?"

"Yes," LuAnn said. "As soon as he gets back to us."

When the door closed behind the mechanic, LuAnn and Tess turned their heads simultaneously and stared at the bag sitting against the wall. "It does look expensive, doesn't it?" LuAnn said.

Tess nodded. "I'd say designer, if I had to guess."

<hr>

"Where should we go for lunch?" LuAnn asked a full hour later as they pulled out of Hilltop Auto. It had taken Ed Baxter almost forty-five minutes to finish his phone call. When he came back into the customer area of the shop, he blinked in surprise. Clearly, he'd forgotten they were even there.

"I'm in the mood for pizza," LuAnn said.

Tess nodded. "Over the Moon sounds fabulous." She glanced at her phone, flat in her palm, on speaker. "Does that sound okay to you, Janice?"

Stacy had picked up Larry a few minutes earlier, so Janice was free to join them for lunch. "It sounds perfect," she said over the phone. "I'm starving. Poor Larry can't keep a thing on his stomach, and I didn't have the heart to eat in front of him."

They met up a few minutes later, pulling into the parking lot almost at the same time. LuAnn's phone rang as Tess slid from the seat.

Janice waved and smiled, and they met in front of the door. Janice talked about the morning's happenings at the inn while they waited for LuAnn to finish her call. "Willa O'Hara called before I left. She's driving Winnie crazy with changes to the menu for the birthday party." Janice shook her head. "Poor Winnie. It was supposed to be an informal little birthday party with finger foods and birthday cake with family and a few friends. Now it's becoming something of a circus with Karl Mannus doing coverage for TV."

Tess didn't have time to say much more than "Poor Winnie" before LuAnn walked up, stuffing her phone into her purse.

"That was Robin. She just wanted to let us know she got the newspaper ad placed for the Easter EGGstravaganza. It'll start running day after tomorrow."

The server greeted them and beckoned them to follow her to their seat.

Janice grinned as they settled into a booth. "Larry can't wait until the Easter egg hunt. Of course, he knows that Jesus is the true reason we celebrate Easter, but he's not one to turn down chocolate or jelly beans."

"My grands as well. Lizzie's been cutting them back from sweets, afraid Henry's getting a little pudgy. I had to show her photos to prove to her what a chunky baby and toddler she was before I was able to get her to simmer down and realize he'll thin out and fatten back up ten times before he's five."

Janice nodded. "Exactly. Give the babies their Easter candy." The server returned with glasses of water, and they ordered. After the server walked away, Janice focused on Tess. "I take it Ed's got your car?"

Tess took a sip of her water. "I'll pick it up in a couple of days." She cast a glance at LuAnn, who was already leaning on her elbows, obviously anxious to spill the beans. She told Janice about the bag at Ed's place.

"Why didn't you two just bring it back to the inn to save Titus the trip?" Janice asked. "No one is going to think we'd steal it."

"The thought never crossed my mind," said Tess.

"Mine either," LuAnn said. "Dane, the mechanic—you know him, Janice—who works for Ed, told us he peeked inside the suitcases they took from the car right after the accident."

"I'm not sure I'd be admitting that," Janice said, her eyes creasing with amusement. "But what did he find?"

"Unless he's fibbing just to tease us," LuAnn said, "one of them was full of money. Tons of it."

A little gasp escaped Janice. "Do you think Titus robbed a bank?"

"I suppose that's one explanation," LuAnn said. "But he doesn't seem the type." She smiled at the server, who brought three salads and cokes and set them on the table in front of them.

"Have you ever met a bank robber?" Janice challenged.

LuAnn grinned as she slid her straw into her glass. "Good point. Let's bless the food so we can eat."

They bowed their heads while LuAnn said a quick heartfelt blessing.

"What's the bag still doing at Ed's anyway?" Janice asked, lifting her head and diving right back into the conversation.

Tess filled her in between bites of salad.

"I wonder if he'll ever mention the money to us," Janice mused.

The server returned, carrying their pizza. They suspended the conversation while she served them each a slice. "Anything else I can get for you ladies?"

"I think we're just fine, hon," Janice said. She glanced around the dining room, which had filled up in the last few minutes. "It looks like you're starting to get busy. Don't worry too much about us. We're just going to eat and gab a little."

When she'd gone, Tess returned to the topic at hand. "Why on earth would Titus want to tell us one of his bags is filled with money? We're practically strangers."

"Oh, I don't know." Janice shrugged. "He seems pretty forthcoming so far."

Tess had to admit that was the truth. She hadn't even had the chance to tell her two friends about the conversation she'd had with Titus in the library room the night before. "Titus seems to be truly worried about what he'll find out about himself."

"What do you mean?" LuAnn asked.

"I found him in the library when I was locking up last night."

"That's right," LuAnn said. "Huck went out about ten, and Titus was reading. I swear, he must be a dog whisperer, or something. Huck didn't want to leave him. What did Titus say that makes you think he's worried?"

"He thinks he must not have been a very good man if no one has put in a missing person's report. He seems to think if he was a father, he must not have been a very good one."

"I find that hard to believe. He seems so gentle and kind," Janice said. "I know we don't really know him, but we're pretty good judges of character, and you can't fake gentleness of the eyes. And Huck likes him so much."

"Speaking of Huck," LuAnn said. "Do we know when we can pick him up?"

"Sally said this afternoon." Tess reached into her purse and pulled out her phone and the card she'd gotten from the groomer. "She said there's a link we can go to if we want to keep an eye on him."

Janice grinned. "Oh, let's do it!"

They scanned the camera angles until they located Huck. "There he is!" LuAnn said. "And look, he's all trimmed and bathed. Doesn't that bandana around his neck look adorable?"

Tess pointed at the screen. "Looks like he made a little friend." Huck was running with a long-haired Chihuahua. "Maybe we need to have puppy play dates or something."

The three of them passed the phone back and forth for a couple of minutes, laughing as the two dogs dodged in and out, nipping at each other. Finally, with reluctance, Tess put her phone back in her purse. "I'll call the shop when we're finished eating," she said. "Can one of you take me by Western Union to verify the money order Titus gave us?"

LuAnn signaled the server for a refill of her soda. "I can," she said.

Janice gave a snort. "With all that cash he was carrying around, I doubt he conjured up a bogus money order."

It did seem unlikely, but better safe than sorry.

They finished their meal and left a generous tip for their busy server, then went their separate ways in the parking lot— Janice back to the inn and Tess and LuAnn headed toward Western Union, where Tess verified the money order, before swinging by the groomer to retrieve Huck. He shook, barked, and whined again all the way back to the inn. Once they set him down in the foyer, he took off, lickety-split, up the stairs. LuAnn shook her head. "I wonder why he's so upset about the car."

"Maybe it's the crate," Tess said.

"I'd best go see about him, make sure he goes all the way up to our rooms." LuAnn headed toward the stairs. "The event planner will be here in a few minutes. Everything is almost set for the big day."

"I'll let you know when she arrives."

The Easter EGGstravaganza was a first-annual community event that Tess, Janice, and LuAnn hoped and prayed would bless the children of Marietta and provide a safe and free day of fun, food, prizes, and, of course, candy. Many of the games and inflatables, like the bouncy house and ball pit, had been donated, and the fire department and police department were collecting and donating candy for the egg hunt.

A flash of yellow caught Tess's attention just as she was about to walk toward the café to help with cleanup. She turned, glancing out the front window. Titus Jones was struggling to get out of a cab. Leaning heavily on his cane, he met the driver at the back of the car. He carried the small black bag they'd seen at Ed's earlier.

She opened the door and went out to meet him.

He struggled to carry the obviously heavy bag with his free hand.

"Let me help you with that, Titus."

"It's pretty heavy, but I think I can manage, thank you, Tess."

As she trailed a little behind their mysterious guest, Tess wondered if Titus had already looked inside the bag or if he was about to learn something new about himself. Would something from his past trigger his memories? Was it possible that, by the end of the day, Titus Jones would, at the very least, be catching glimpses of who he was before his accident?

And, if so, would he be happy with the man he discovered, or would he discover he wasn't the man he wanted to be?

CHAPTER FIVE

Tess sat back in her chair, mulling over the events of the day. All afternoon she'd kept a watchful eye toward the stairs and elevator, hoping Titus would emerge and address the contents of the bag, but as far as she could tell, he hadn't ventured downstairs even once.

She heaved a deep sigh just as a tap on the office door caught her attention. Robin peeked in. "Tess? Sorry to bother you. I can't find LuAnn or Janice, and there's a delivery guy here. He wants to know where to unload the boxes."

"Boxes?" Tess stood.

Robin shrugged. "I don't know what they are, but there's a lot of them."

"Where is he?"

"At the front desk."

Tess greeted the delivery man with a tentative smile. "I'm Tess Wallace. What do you have for us?"

"Twenty boxes." He showed her the order form.

"Okay. Take them around to the loading dock, if you don't mind. We'll have to leave them there until we figure out where to put them."

"Yes, ma'am," he said.

"Well?" Robin said after he left. "What on earth is in that truck that took twenty boxes to ship?"

"The plastic eggs for the Easter egg hunt. Six thousand of them."

Robin's jaw dropped, then a wide grin stretched her lips. "I suppose I know what we're all going to be doing in our spare time for the next week."

"I'd better go show him exactly where to put the boxes so he doesn't block the back kitchen door."

"I'll go with you," Robin said. "Winnie's starting to practice and taste test hors d'oeuvres for Molly O'Hara's birthday party. I told her earlier that I'd help for a little while after I get off. Which is just about now."

The kitchen was starting to smell of bacon and fish and other delectable but unidentified aromas as they entered. Winnie stood over the big red stove that held three large skillets. She held a platter in one hand and metal tongs in the other. Janice stood by the door with her hands on her hips. "What on earth is that delivery man unloading?" she asked Tess over her shoulder.

"Those are the plastic eggs for the Easter egg hunt. They'll all have to be filled with candy and little prizes before next Friday so we can get them placed before Saturday when the kids start showing up."

"How many?"

"Six thousand."

"Goodness gracious goat."

Winnie joined them at the back door, wiping her hands on the edge of her apron. "Why'd you order so many?"

"We already have two hundred kids signed up online, and that was just from the flyers we put up around town two weeks ago. With the newspaper ad coming out tomorrow, I'm sure we'll have several hundred more."

Though the event was free, the event planner had suggested having people sign up so that children and their parents could be issued wristbands with matching numbers.

"Where are we going to keep them in the meantime?"

As it turned out, the twenty boxes weren't excessively large, so storage didn't present the problem Tess had envisioned.

Winnie moved away from the door and back to the stove. "Better not put them in a common area where guests might trip and hurt themselves. That's a lawsuit waiting to happen."

Tess hated to be cynical, but Winnie wasn't wrong on that point. "The office has two free corners, so we can stack five boxes in each corner for now. I suppose the other ten can go upstairs in our apartment. We don't want to leave them outside, in case it rains again."

Janice opened the door as the delivery truck drove away. "Let's get moving."

They each grabbed a box, and when they reached the foyer, Karl and Shyla Mannus were just walking through the door. "Ladies, what are you doing?"

Karl took the box from Janice's arms without asking.

"Oh, they're just plastic eggs." Janice smiled at him. "They hardly weigh anything at all." She laughed. "A lot less than my grandson, I can tell you that."

"Still, I insist." Karl flashed her his extra-white smile.

Shyla held out her arms toward Tess. "Let me."

Tess chuckled inwardly. Apparently, these two considered them little old ladies.

"Now, where are we going with these?" Karl asked.

"Follow me," Tess said as the phone rang. Janice walked around the counter to answer. She gave a little wave as she picked up the receiver.

Tess led the duo into the office and pointed to the corners. "We're going to stack them here for now."

Karl set his box where Tess instructed and, turning, took Shyla's to stack on top of it. "Are there more?"

Tess grinned. "Twenty in all." How committed was Karl to this good deed? "But we're only putting ten in here."

To his credit, Karl didn't even blink. Instead he rubbed his hands together good-humoredly. "Point me to the rest."

Though she was impressed with this more relaxed, on-vacation Karl she'd never really seen before, Tess shook her head. "Oh, Karl. We can get them. We don't normally call on our guests to haul delivery boxes for us."

"I'd like to think I'm more than a guest by now. I've done enough stories on the inn that I feel like we're old friends."

Did he really? This leopard was changing his spots awfully quickly. Unless he was simply happier when his wife was around.

"Okay, if you insist, they're on the loading dock, just off the kitchen. I'll show you." Tess didn't allow her surprise to show at his statement, nor at the fact that he seemed genuine. She'd always kept her guard up around the TV news reporter. It only seemed reasonable to do so. She turned to address Shyla. "What have the two of you been up to today? Have you seen any of the historical sites?"

"Just one, so far." Shyla looked askance at her husband, but her eyes held amusement.

"We staked out the O'Hara mansion." Karl's long strides overtook Tess, and he reached the kitchen first. He pushed open the door and hung back for the two women to precede him.

As they stepped inside, the savory smells of Winnie's delicious cooking assailed their senses. The table was laden with the preparations for the birthday party. LuAnn and Robin had joined Winnie at the stove.

Janice followed them into the kitchen. "I can only imagine how busy everything is over there with the party Friday night."

Shyla nodded. "That's why Karl couldn't get in the door to speak with Mrs. O'Hara. So we just sat in the car across the street and watched everything that was going on."

"That must've been fun," Tess said wryly.

"More fun than you might think." Shyla laughed. "We even ate convenience-store hotdogs and chips. It was almost like a picnic with binoculars."

"Any leads on the big O'Hara exposé?"

Karl walked back inside from the loading dock carrying a box. He gave her a wide grin. "You'll just have to wait and find out like everyone else." Shyla held out her arms for the box, and he complied, then brought in another.

"Let me take that one, Karl," Tess said. "It'll take fewer trips if I help out."

Robin stepped over to them, wiping her hands on a towel. "Tess, I'll trade places with you and help Karl and Shyla load the boxes in the office. Winnie needs tasters for her fancy hors d'oeuvres, and to tell you the truth, everything is starting to taste like scallops to me. Even the shrimp puffs."

Janice nodded. "Even this pâté is starting to taste fishy."

"No one's complained about my cooking before," Winnie said, her shoulders squaring as she stood over the stove.

"Oh, Winnie! It's delicious," Janice said. "Every single bite. But you have to admit, we've been tasting a lot of different flavors."

"Get yourself some lemon water to cleanse your palate. The crab cakes are done."

"Save me one," Robin said as she, Karl, and Shyla walked out the door.

Tess grabbed an appetizer plate from the table. "What do you need me to try?"

Winnie pointed her toward the table. "Just start eating. Tell me which ones taste fancy enough for those O'Haras."

"How many different appetizers are you planning to serve?" Tess grabbed a dumpling and dipped it in the sauce in the center of the plate. "Mmm. This pork dumpling is divine." It wasn't exactly "fancy," but just because someone lives in a mansion doesn't mean they can't appreciate simple, delicious food.

"Thank you," Winnie said. "Keep tasting."

Tess filled her plate with a variety of finger foods—some elegant, some less elegant but equally delicious. Janice shoved back her plate and shook her head. "I'm sorry, Winnie. I can't eat one more bite. But the crab cakes are wonderful. You're the absolute Midas of food." She turned her attention to Tess. "Try that cream tartlet."

Tess reached for one. With her plate full, she leaned against the counter and dug in.

"So, Karl is being helpful," Janice said.

"Yes. And his wife is darling." Tess smiled. "They had a picnic in the car while they staked out the comings and goings at Molly O'Hara's today. She seemed to have a great time."

Janice smiled. "Do you think anything will come of Karl digging into the O'Haras?"

Tess shrugged. "Doubtful. You know we've been hearing those rumors forever, and no one's ever come out with any proof. Mostly, I'd say it's all sensationalism, probably because the O'Haras are wealthy, and no one actually knows where their money came from."

LuAnn set another plate on the table with three types of dip and various crackers to go with them. "He did find that connection between them and that mob family in New York. It's possible that Karl might finally be the one to uncover the key to their wealth after all these years of speculation."

"Is it really anyone's business?" Winnie asked, setting a plate of golden-brown crab cakes on the table.

"No," LuAnn said. "But when has that ever stopped curiosity?"

———— ⚜ ————

Later, Tess sat in the fourth-floor common room she shared with her two friends. Taylor had hauled the other ten boxes to their apartment, via the elevator, and they now filled every empty space of their common area. One box of plastic eggs sat on the floor next to Tess's chair. On the table in front of her were packages of candy. She reached for a plastic egg and looked across at LuAnn, sitting in a chair with her notebook in hand. LuAnn spoke aloud as she wrote. "Titus Jones: Who is he? Where is he from?" LuAnn processed through the written word. Her penchant for scribbling and scratching had been their saving grace more than once in their long friendship. And more recently, LuAnn's ability to keep track of clues and details had helped them solve a few mysteries surrounding the inn.

She stopped with her pen poised above the page and pursed her lips, her eyes narrowing as she stared pensively at the notebook.

"What is it, LuAnn?" Janice asked. She sat on the couch, an empty laundry basket at her feet, which would hold the filled Easter eggs.

Huck seemed none the worse for wear after his ordeal in the car and was curled up next to Janice. Their cat, Tom, Huck's stray sidekick, sat on Janice's other side as she stroked him absently.

"I was just thinking about Karl staking out the O'Hara house earlier when there's no evidence to suggest anything criminal or shady about them other than rumor. It makes me wonder if we even have the right to look into Titus's past since we don't have any evidence that he's done anything wrong."

"I hear you." Tess nodded. "At what point does 'helping' become 'prying'?"

"Karl might be onto something," Janice said. "He did say he found a connection between Molly O'Hara and the Kelly family in New York. And the Bickerton sisters confirmed it at lunch yesterday."

"But that doesn't have anything at all to do with Titus. And I don't want him to feel like we don't trust him." LuAnn expelled a breath. "Should we table the whole thing? He's paid up for a month."

Janice shook her head. "Don't you think he might appreciate our efforts to help him discover his identity? He seems desperate to find out the truth."

The memory of Titus's face the night before as he wondered what sort of man he used to be flickered across Tess's mind. "I for one would love to be able to set his mind at ease that he was just as good before he lost his memory as he seems to be now."

Tess glanced at LuAnn and raised a questioning brow. LuAnn hesitated, then shrugged. "It wouldn't hurt to make a list. What do we already know?"

"He has amnesia," Janice said.

"That goes without saying," LuAnn said, but she wrote it down anyway.

Tess reached for a bag of candy from the coffee table. "Unless he doesn't." She twisted open a pastel blue egg and filled it with a couple of bite-sized chocolate bars before popping the two halves together again.

"Why would you say that?" Janice asked. "Especially when you're the one who just said you want to put his mind at ease."

Tess shrugged. "I'm just asking the question. Especially since he brought a suitcase full of cash into this inn."

"But he probably doesn't know where that came from any more than we do," Janice said. "Who in his right mind would carry around a suitcase full of money? It doesn't make any sense in the normal world, does it? There has to be something going on." The question hung in the air between them, not focused toward anyone in particular.

"You're right," Tess acknowledged. "Still, all things considered, the way he booked his room initially without a credit card, an address that doesn't exist, a story about being widowed that would tug at anyone's heartstrings..."

Janice heaved a sigh. "So, you think there's something that's not on the up-and-up about him?"

"I don't know about that. You and I might not be inclined to lie in order to hide our identities, but it's not criminal if that's what he did," Tess said. "But the point is, if he's telling the truth about his amnesia, he doesn't know where that money came from either. He wouldn't even remember if he's a criminal. His memory could come back any time, and we'd never know if he didn't tell us."

LuAnn made a note on the page in her lap. "I think what you're saying, Tess, is that Titus could regain his memory at any time. And if he came by his wealth nefariously, and suddenly remembers he's a thief or worse, we could all be in danger, and so could our guests."

Janice nodded thoughtfully. "I didn't think about that. I just find it hard to believe he's lying. And I'd still like to try to track down who he is or at least who he was before he lost his memory." She shooed both animals off the couch and reached for a bag of candy. "Do you think it's possible that someone could be a criminal and then lose his memory of the past and no longer be evil?"

It was a compelling question, but one for which Tess couldn't even venture a guess. "I don't think that's a question anyone but God can answer with certainty."

"Okay." LuAnn tapped her pen on her notebook. "Let's start from the very beginning." She turned her gaze on Tess. "What do you remember from the day he made the reservation? Before the accident, when he still had his memories."

"Just what I've already mentioned. He said he was trying to get some time away from well-meaning friends and family so that he could mourn his wife in peace."

"Poor man," Janice said. "And he doesn't even remember her. At least Tess and I have wonderful memories of our husbands."

Tess nodded. "I can't imagine how awful it would feel to be in his position. Not knowing if he has children and grandchildren." Although she couldn't help but wonder why he would need to get away if he had family to gather around him for comfort. She never would have survived those first awful weeks without Jeff Jr. and Lizzie and Lizzie's husband, Michael.

"Can you imagine how it must plague his mind that he can't find any information about himself?" Janice reached over and claimed another handful of candy. She dropped it in her lap and began to fill the eggs. "It's as though he never existed."

"So, to recap what we know…" LuAnn's eyes drifted back to her notebook. "Titus was looking to get away and then"—she wrote on the page—"he was in an accident on his way here."

"And now his mind is a blank slate," Janice chimed in.

"Allegedly," LuAnn said again.

"I know there's a chance he's faking," Janice said. "But like I said, I feel like he's telling the truth." She twisted another egg apart and slid a single-serving package of jelly beans inside, then popped the two pieces of plastic back together. "I mean, he's definitely not lying about the accident or the four months he's been recovering. Those are verifiable."

"That's true." LuAnn twisted her lips in contemplation and made another note. "Is it possible he lost his memory initially, but has regained it now? Like Tess said, how would we know? It's been four whole months."

"To what end, though?" Janice set four filled eggs in the laundry basket at her feet.

Tess hated to shake Janice's faith in Titus, especially when she herself was split about his intentions.

LuAnn grabbed a small package of jelly beans. "I can see both sides. It's possible Titus is exactly who he claims to be, a man who has completely lost his memory and, because he didn't let anyone know he was leaving, his tracks are so well covered that even his own family can't find him after all these months." She opened the candy and popped one in her mouth.

"Exactly my point," Janice said. She gave LuAnn a stern look over her glasses. "And those are for the children."

"I know. I'm sorry. You know I love the red ones." She popped another into her mouth, then returned to the topic. "Everyone has some sort of fingerprint somewhere. And I don't mean actual fingerprints," she said, with a pointed look at Janice, the most literal of the three of them. "Wouldn't there be some trace of him somewhere?"

"You know," Tess said, suddenly feeling the urge to play devil's advocate, "there's another possibility we haven't considered that would explain why he paid without a credit card and why he has all that money."

LuAnn pursed her lips and held her pen over the notebook, ready to scribble something they might be able to use. "What do you mean, Tess?"

"What if, for instance, he's working for the FBI or CIA? Maybe he was coming here to investigate some criminal."

"And he needed a suitcase full of money to accomplish the task?"

"Maybe he would, if..." Janice turned a little red.

"What?" LuAnn asked.

"Promise you won't laugh."

"Of course," Tess said.

"What if he was coming to this area to pay a ransom—you know the FBI gets involved with kidnapping cases—and his accident cost someone his or her life? Or"—her eyes went wider—"what if he was the kidnapper, and the money is the ransom he collected?"

Janice looked at Tess, then LuAnn, then back to Tess. "Too much *Law and Order*, right?"

"Not necessarily," LuAnn said. "I'm just mulling it over."

"No," Janice said. "I guess that's not really rational. And it would mean he's not really from New Jersey, right? He wouldn't be involved in a kidnapping in Ohio if he were from New Jersey, would he?"

"It makes as much sense as Titus being a government agent in the first place," Tess said. "A ransom would definitely explain the suitcase of money. But I don't remember hearing anything on the news about a kidnapping, do you?"

"No, but you know who I bet might remember something like that?" LuAnn popped another jelly bean in her mouth.

"Karl," Tess said. "If a kidnaping was made public, I suppose he would know."

LuAnn nodded. "If he reported on anything like that, he'd remember. You know he works closely with the police in several towns, including Marietta." She bit the inside of her lip and narrowed her gaze as she looked at Tess.

"What are you thinking?" Tess asked.

"You know who else might know something more than local police would?"

Tess knew she was thinking about their FBI agent friend, Charles Butler. "I thought about him. But he'd ask even more questions than Karl, and we might have to tell him about Titus having the bag of money. I'd hate to throw unnecessary suspicion on Titus."

Janice shifted and grabbed another bag of plastic eggs. "On the other hand, what if Titus is the missing piece of the puzzle, and we could give Agent Butler what he needs to solve an open case?" Her mouth suddenly made an *O*, and her eyes widened. "What if Titus is in WITSEC like Ellie and Marsha last month?"

LuAnn shook her head with a frown. "Isn't that a little too coincidental?"

Janice sniffed. "If this were a movie, maybe. We wouldn't want the same plot in the sequel, but this is real life. And Charles did say the FBI looks for inns like ours with owners like us to hold people safely until they can testify."

"Janice might have a point." LuAnn shrugged. "Except he doesn't have a memory, so how could he testify?"

"Unless that's his cover," Tess argued. "And anyway, if that's the case, the government already knows who he is and where he is."

Janice could be like a dog with a bone sometimes. But if she was right, that would explain a few unanswered questions about Titus. Agent Butler had come into their lives months ago. He had helped them during a couple of their mysteries. But Tess didn't want to take advantage of him.

LuAnn wrote in her notebook. "I suppose it wouldn't hurt to at least put in a call to him. We need to invite his twins to the Easter egg hunt anyway."

Janice brightened. "Oh, good idea."

Tess hadn't even thought about inviting Charles and his wife and twins to the Easter EGGstravaganza. She'd have to give him a call.

Janice pressed the back of her hand to her mouth, covering a wide yawn. She stuffed the two empty plastic bags into the box and set the laundry basket on the couch. "That's about it for me. I'm heading to bed. There's a documentary about the Lindbergh baby on Amazon Prime. All this talk about kidnapping and ransoms. I might watch that. Maybe it'll give me some ideas about this case."

After Janice's door closed behind her, LuAnn capped her pen and closed her notebook. "Do you really think Titus might be FBI?"

"I don't know." Tess stood, gathering the eggs she'd filled and adding them to the basket Janice had started. "But if we're going to figure out where he came from, we have to start somewhere. If he's not FBI, maybe Karl or Charles will have some information about a missing person that matches his description or a crime that will take us to the next clue."

"Maybe." LuAnn set aside her pen and notebook and stood. Huck bounded up instantly and ran to the door. "I guess I better take him out before I turn in."

"Hang on," Tess said. "I'll come with you."

LuAnn held Huck's leash as they descended the steps from the fourth floor. When they reached the third floor landing, Tess saw the soft glow of light coming from under Titus's door. "Have you seen Titus since he picked up his bag?" she whispered.

LuAnn shook her head. "I haven't. Do you think he's avoiding us?"

"Why would he? It's not like he knows Dane told us about the money."

"Unless Dane mentioned it to him today when he picked up his bag."

"That would explain it." A sudden thought occurred to Tess as they reached the first floor and started to walk toward the front door. "You don't think..."

"What?" LuAnn asked.

"Do you think he left?"

"You mean *left* left? Like he snuck out all tippy-toe in the middle of the afternoon?"

"I don't know, maybe. Has anyone seen him since he got back to the inn with his bag?"

"He ordered takeout for dinner tonight."

"He did? I didn't know that." Of course, she hadn't thought to ask. "Then he was here through supper, at least."

"Huck!" LuAnn scolded the pup when he pulled so suddenly she dropped the leash. He took off at a sprint. "Huck!"

"It's okay, ladies," a man's voice said as a tall figure stepped from the shadows. "I have him."

That answered the question whether Titus was still at the inn or not. But there were so many more. The main question on Tess's mind at the moment was, did Titus want to answer those questions, or keep the truth locked away in the dark places of his hidden memory?

CHAPTER SIX

Karl and Shyla were sitting in the café over half-eaten breakfasts when Tess entered the room the next morning. They were each engaged in their own activity as they ate. Shyla rumpled a local newspaper while Karl's laptop sat open just off to the side of his plate—which Tess found a little dangerous, for the computer's sake.

She walked to the coffee bar and filled a cup with a bold-flavored something or other Winnie had put out, then walked toward the couple. Shyla glanced up and flashed Tess a smile as she approached.

"You two are up and about early." Tess stood next to the table as Karl kept his focus on his computer screen.

"Karl wanted an early start." Shyla's eyes gleamed with pride as she glanced at her husband. "That's why he's displaying the manners of a goat at the moment, right honey?"

Karl glanced up, blinking, then seemed to come back to earth as he cast his gaze upward to Tess. He used his foot to shove out an empty chair. "Sorry. I get caught up. Will you sit?"

"I will, thank you." Tess dropped into the chair and took a sip of her coffee. Then she set her cup on the table and reached for a packet of sugar. "So, what are your big plans for the day that got you out of bed so early?"

"Karl snagged a face-to-face interview with Molly O'Hara."

"Really?" Tess stirred her coffee, glancing at Shyla and then Karl over the rim of her cup. "I thought you were going to speak with her Friday at the party."

"He wasn't supposed to do a formal interview. Just report on the party itself and talk to the guests. You know, ask questions like, how long have you known the honoree, that sort of thing. The O'Haras sent him a bio and photos for the background story. But when the police officer talked to us last night…"

"Wait, you got pulled over?"

Karl grinned. "No. We went back to the O'Haras' after dinner."

"For another stakeout," Shyla pitched in. "I don't know if the officer just noticed our car was there twice in one day, or if someone reported us."

"Should've rented a black car," Karl muttered.

Shyla nodded, her eyes glinting with amusement. "Or an SUV like on all the crime TV shows."

Tess chuckled at the pair. Shyla was clearly enjoying the process of getting the big story. But Tess wasn't so sure about Karl. He seemed…tense.

Seemingly undaunted by Karl's distracted mood, Shyla smiled with a quick eyebrow raise. "Turns out, the officer who caught us watching the house is Mrs. O'Hara's grandson."

"Oh, Sergeant Johnny O'Hara. Of course."

"You know him?" Shyla asked as Tess took a sip of coffee.

Nodding, Tess set her cup back on the table. "He's an intimidating man. I wouldn't have wanted to be caught spying on his grandmother's home."

"He was tough at first, but he eased up when Karl showed his credentials and told him that he's the one covering the party tomorrow night."

"And he said he'd fix it so I can go in this morning and have a sit-down with Mrs. O'Hara."

"He told us she has a lot of stories that would be great for her birthday party article."

"That was a lucky break," Tess said.

"I don't believe in luck. We all make our own success," Karl said. "If we're willing to do what it takes."

"God helps those who help themselves?" Tess offered a wry smile. "As long as their wives don't mind spending half of their tenth-anniversary trip chasing a story."

Shyla leaned in a little toward Tess, resting her arms on the table. "It's more fun than I ever expected. And who knows what might happen if the right people see his story."

"Well," Karl said. "A story about an elderly lady's birthday won't get much attention, but if that elderly lady happens to be the widow of a mob boss..." He shrugged. "Maybe."

Tess knew from past experience with Karl that he was dedicated to his profession, but she'd never really considered whether he had bigger ambitions. She hated to rain on his parade, so she refrained from mentioning that it was unlikely he would discover anything beneath the surface about the family. Others had tried and come up short—and not for lack of trying. She'd heard of everything: reporters going through the O'Haras' trash, taking photos through their windows, even breaking in and going through the house. Tess felt a little sorry for the family being under such scrutiny all because they were wealthy and a bit eccentric. At the end of the day, they did have a right to their privacy. Tess realized the irony of that thought when just last night she and her friends were discussing Titus. Which reminded her...

"Karl, I'm glad you're here early. I actually have a question for you."

"I heard about your big community"—his fingers curled in the "air quotes" sign— "'EGGstravaganza.' I assume you want coverage?"

Fighting the urge to give him an air quote "no," Tess smiled instead. "We certainly wouldn't turn down the publicity, but that's not it." She shifted in her chair and smiled as Robin stopped by to fill their cups. When she walked away, Tess leaned forward and dropped her tone.

"Okay, do you happen to remember if you maybe did a kidnapping story in the past few months where a ransom was involved? It would've been sometime around Thanksgiving."

In a split second, Karl's expression morphed from slightly distracted by whatever was on his computer screen to fully engaged. "A kidnapping?"

"Something the FBI might have solved or thwarted?" Though, if Janice's theory about the kidnapping and ransom was right, there was a chance it hadn't been met with a very good outcome, considering Titus still had the money in his possession.

Karl frowned as though searching his memory, then shook his head. "No, I'd remember something like that. But if it was a high-profile kidnapping that involved the FBI, we wouldn't have been brought in until after the fact. They wouldn't want to tip off the kidnappers or the public to an operation like that."

"I suppose that's true." And that was that. If Titus was in the accident on his way to pay a ransom, the full deal had never gone through. Besides, the more she thought about it, the more she knew it wasn't logical. Whether he was a kidnapper or a person paying ransom, the police would have been aware of the payoff and would have followed the money. His identity at the accident scene wouldn't have been a mystery to them. So, the best thing she could do was to put in that call to Agent Butler as soon as possible and ask him about their other ideas. "Thank you for your time. I won't keep you any longer. But good luck with the interview."

"Wait a second." He closed his computer and reached for the sugar. "I have some time before we have to leave for the O'Haras' house. Tell me why you want to know about a kidnapping."

Tess hesitated, searching her mind for anything to throw him off the scent. The truth was, if Karl was so determined to find a story about the O'Haras when there was really nothing to link the family to anything notorious, what would he do with Titus? An amnesiac who discovered a suitcase filled with tens of thousands or hundreds of thousands of dollars would most likely be an even tastier morsel—too juicy to pass up. She decided to head him off, if possible. "It's nothing, really. Janice and LuAnn and I were thinking there might have been one at the end of November, and I saw you having your breakfast." She gave him her best, most winning smile. "I figured if anyone would know, you would."

He furrowed his brow as he clearly went into investigative mode. "But what prompted you to think such a thing? It couldn't have been just random musing." His gaze darted to the doorway, and his expression lit up. He waved. Tess hoped against hope that he was distracted.

"Good morning, you two." Tess closed her eyes at the unmistakable sound of Janice's voice. "How's the coffee? Winnie said she was going to brew that delicious hazelnut blend along with the regular coffee."

"She did brew some, and you're right. It is delicious," Shyla said with a welcoming smile. "Whipped cream too." She glanced at Karl. "My husband is a purist. Only regular coffee, strong enough to hold up a stick right in the middle of the cup."

Karl laughed, though his gaze on Tess told her that he hadn't given up on the kidnapping thread. "Will you join us, Janice?"

Janice glanced around the nearly empty café. "I certainly will. Until it picks up anyway. Thank you. How's the week going for you two? I'm so glad the weather cooperated." She smiled as Robin headed their way carrying a cup and saucer. She and Tess would have their breakfast, then help as the café got busier. Trying to help right now would be too many cooks in the kitchen. "After that sleet on Tuesday, I was afraid we were in for a last blast of winter."

Janice stood and walked to the coffee bar.

"What time is your interview with Molly?" Tess asked.

Shyla put her coffee cup down. "Not until eight thirty."

When Janice returned a minute later, she looked around the table. "What did I miss?"

Karl spoke up quickly, before Tess could divert attention to the interview. "Tess was asking me about a kidnapping story I might have reported a few months ago. But I don't remember anything like that. What made you even think that?"

Janice glanced at Tess. Tess averted her gaze, hoping her friend would catch her drift and not divulge anything to Karl.

"Oh, goodness gracious goat. Are you talking about the Lindbergh docudrama I was telling you about last night, Tess?" She glanced at Karl with a dramatic shiver. "Never watch anything like that before bedtime. The nightmares were terrifying. I just kept seeing Larry, my grandson..." She shuddered. "I'm telling you, just don't do it."

Tess stared at Janice, admiring her quick thinking. And she certainly had talked about watching the movie about the Lindbergh baby.

"The Lindbergh baby?" Karl squinted at Janice. "That's not what it seemed like Tess was asking about."

"Oh, that," Janice said nervously.

That would never throw Karl off the scent. Tess figured they'd have to downplay the subject and hope for the best. "Karl doesn't remember anything about a kidnapping in November."

Disappointment clouded Janice's eyes. "We were just wondering..."

"But again, ladies, why would you?" Karl pressed.

If he showed this sort of tenacity in his interview with Molly, he might just get that big mob story he seemed to crave. Just when Tess thought they were going to have to either tell him about Titus or plead the fifth, his wife seemed to note their discomfiture and came to the rescue.

Shyla reached forward and placed a slim hand over Karl's. "Honey, don't you need to finish your interview questions for the O'Haras?"

He frowned at her obvious attempt to distract him. "Sure. I guess I do."

Tess stood. "We'll take our coffee to a different table so you can work."

"Oh, ladies," Shyla said, quickly. "I didn't mean to imply—"

"No," Tess said. "We insist. Karl, thank you for answering my question."

"That was a close one," Janice whispered as they walked to a nearby table.

"It sure was. He has a big nose for news."

"I'm afraid if we'd stayed there much longer, I'd have caved about Titus. And that's not our story to tell."

April, 6, 1863

Prudence's heart twisted in pity as the boy wolfed down a third helping of stew and thick slices of bread. She feared the food would come right back up, but she didn't have the heart to suggest he stop when he clearly hadn't eaten anything of substance in who knew how long.

So far, the child had not spoken a word. But upon closer inspection of his face and eyes, she'd come to the conclusion that he was anywhere between six and eight. Likely closer to the latter, considering he had made it on his own for a long time.

"The boy's bath is ready, and I laid out Moses's extra set of clothing." Moses was not quite four, but he was big for his age, so his clothes, while they would be a little short, would be acceptable until she could sew the boy a set of his own.

At the mention of a bath, the child looked up, his eyes wide and tinged with a hint of fear.

"Do not worry," Prudence said with a gentle smile. "A warm bath will help thee feel better after such a journey. I promise." At least she assumed he'd been on a journey. She'd certainly never seen him or that dog anywhere near these parts. Hopefully, his lack of conversation was due to self-preservation and not a permanent condition. They needed to know from whence he'd come if they were to help him.

He pushed back his empty bowl and gulped down a glass of milk. His sigh of contentment brought a sting to Prudence's eyes, and she forced back the tears that had threatened to fall since bringing the child into her home.

"Come," Jason said. He held out a hand. With resignation, the boy took it and stood on shaky legs. He cast a glance at the door as they walked to the metal tub sitting in front of the fireplace. Prudence half expected him to attempt to bolt, but, thankfully, he continued to hold Jason's hand.

"Well," Prudence said, standing. "I'll just clean this up and give thee some privacy."

As she washed up the dishes, Prudence let the tears flow. "Father," she whispered, "show us Thy plan for this child Thee has brought to our home."

An hour later, Jason emptied the tub of grimy black water. Prudence arranged a pallet on the floor close to the fire with several quilts. The boy had likely been sleeping on the hard ground for weeks, at least, and probably months given his poor condition. He stared at the fire until his eyes grew heavy, and he finally slept, despite the light outside, Moses's chatter, and the groan of the rocking chair. Prudence sat, sewing together pieces of muslin she had cut from one of Jason's shirts. The boy was slightly larger than Moses, and his wrists poked out from the cuffs of the shirt they'd given him to wear.

Jason had taken the cast-off, foul rags the boy had been wearing and built a fire outside to burn them.

When Jason returned to the house, the new shirt was nearly finished, Moses was quietly practicing his letters on a slate tablet, and their guest was snoring softly.

Prudence glanced up at her husband and smiled. Jason's expression remained grim, and Prudence's heart rate picked up speed. "What is it?" she whispered.

Limping across the room, he held out a yellowed, folded paper. Prudence set her sewing in her lap and reached for it. She carefully unfolded the page and, as her eyes scanned over the faded writing, she felt her stomach drop. On what appeared to be a page ripped from a book, a rough map had been drawn over the words. Beginning far south in Mississippi, the rough, hand-drawn lines twisted and turned, with several spots along the way marked with a large X. She covered her mouth with her hand, and her eyes grew wide as she noted the last stop marked with an X. The inn.

How had the child found his way to them if he had no idea they were the ones he was looking for? A sudden shudder seized her body, and chills moved all over her. God clearly had at least one more assignment for them. She glanced at the small boy sleeping in peace and smiled with trembling lips.

The arms of God had led him straight to their door.

CHAPTER SEVEN

Tess wiped down one of the café's four-top tables and gathered a nice tip to deliver to the tip jar. She dropped the dishcloth into the bucket of bleach water and turned just as Titus entered the café. The lunch crowd wasn't excessive today, which was a mercy considering that Winnie was on double duty in the kitchen, keeping up with soup and breads as well as cooking for tomorrow's birthday party.

She hurried to Titus as he took a seat at a bistro table and pulled out a book. His smile seemed genuine as she approached. "I have to be honest, Tess, those smells coming from the kitchen have been driving me a little crazy for the past couple of hours."

"Winnie's cooking for tomorrow night's shindig at the O'Haras'." Tess smiled.

"Shindig?"

"One of the town matriarchs is turning ninety-five. They're having a birthday party for her. And Winnie is catering it."

"Ah, that explains why there have been so many different smells in the inn the last couple of days."

"Yes, we had a tasting yesterday. We ate so much during the day, none of us had much of an appetite for dinner, but it gave her an idea of what to cook for the party."

Titus chuckled.

"Can I get you some lunch?" Tess asked. "We have potato soup and crab bisque on the menu, and you have a choice of sourdough, yeast rolls, or crispy french bread."

He made his choice, including his drink, and Tess walked into the kitchen a minute later to join the bustle of Winnie, LuAnn, and Janice working alongside Robin, Taylor, and a college-aged girl named Lana, the daughter of one of Winnie's friends whom she'd hired just for the party.

"Everything going okay out there, Tess?" Taylor asked.

"Yes, we're not very busy. I just came to get a bowl of potato soup and sourdough bread for Titus."

Janice reached for a bowl. "I'll get it. I already have on the gloves." She smiled. "How does he seem today? Did he say why he was MIA last night?"

"I didn't pry. But LuAnn and I did see him after you went to bed last night."

"You did? You didn't say anything about it this morning." She set a filled bowl on a tray and pulled out a bread basket. "You said sourdough?"

Tess nodded. "We took Huck for a walk, and Titus was coming back to the inn." Tess got a glass and filled it with iced tea.

"Did he say where he'd been?"

"No. And it didn't occur to me to ask."

"It would've occurred to me."

Tess laughed, lifting the tray. "Yes, but you were watching a docudrama about the Lindbergh baby."

"I still wish I hadn't." She walked with Tess to the door. "It was awful." She paused. "I wonder where on earth he was until after dark though."

Winnie breezed by with an aluminum pan of homemade toast points she would cover with pâté the next day. "Maybe he needed a breath of fresh air and didn't want to answer a lot of nosy questions about where he was every minute of the day."

Janice rolled her eyes and pushed open the door for Tess. "You should invite Titus to the party tomorrow night. Maybe his late-night stroll was a cry for help."

Winnie put the pan on the table with a clatter. "I'd say he just wanted to be alone."

"Or," Janice went on, "he was so bored, he left a perfectly warm and cozy room on a cold night because he needed to get out of the inn."

Winnie seemed uncharacteristically stressed with the food prep. "Is Winnie okay?" Tess asked, dropping her volume to a whisper. "She seems cranky."

"Apparently, Willa O'Hara is now expecting one hundred guests, which is about forty more people to cook for than Winnie was originally told. And she just found out this morning. That's why she hired Lana."

"Poor Winnie. But if anyone will pass the test with flying colors, she will. Let's offer to help out tomorrow, if she'll let us."

Tess left the kitchen carrying Titus's lunch. She set down his bowl and bread and tucked the tray under her arm. Janice was right about inviting him to the party. And what was she risking by the invitation? He could always say no if the idea was unappealing.

"Titus, would you be interested in joining Janice and me at a party tomorrow night?" The thought of him being holed up in his room just felt wrong. After all those months in the hospital and a rehab facility, amnesia notwithstanding, he should be enjoying life, not hiding out. A party at one of the most affluent homes in Marietta just seemed a good fit.

She ventured a glance at him and noted a frown creasing his brow. Likely, he was trying to find a polite way to refuse. Maybe he truly preferred to spend time alone in his room. Tess had known plenty of introverts who didn't enjoy social gatherings.

"Please, don't feel you have to accept the invitation. I don't want to impose."

"No, no. I'd be pleased to accept, of course. And thank you for your generosity. But I noticed that you only mentioned you and Janice. LuAnn isn't going?"

Tess smiled. "LuAnn is attending with another friend." Brad Grimes had been LuAnn's plus-one for several months. She insisted they were just friends, though Tess and Janice could both see that their feelings for each other were growing.

LuAnn came into the café shaking her head.

After making sure Titus had everything he needed to enjoy his lunch, Tess met her friend halfway across the dining room. "What's wrong?"

"Nothing. I just needed a breather. Winnie is beside herself. She's got a lot on her shoulders. Especially with the variety of appetizers Willa wants."

"She seems to have it under control."

LuAnn sighed. "It's just that there are certain foods that have to be cooked tomorrow because they don't reheat well."

"Like crab cakes, scallops, and shrimp?"

LuAnn poured a glass of water from one of the pitchers on the wait cart and took two large gulps. "The seafood most definitely has to be done tomorrow. And Willa specifically requested several fish-based hors d'oeuvres." She shook her head. "Janice mentioned that you spoke with Karl this morning."

Tess expelled a sigh. "Yes, he didn't remember anything about a kidnapping or ransom. Besides, I really don't think that's our answer."

Disappointment passed over LuAnn's face. "Do you think it's time for us to place a call to Agent Butler?"

After a busy lunch, Tess retreated to the office and dialed Charles Butler's number. She was surprised when he answered. "Tess?" he said. "What's going on?"

Her heart sped up at the thought of how she would explain why she was asking about Titus if Charles pressed for an answer the way Karl had. "Oh, we wanted to know if you and Rebekah and the twins are coming for the EGGstravaganza next Saturday. I know it's the day before Easter, so you might already have plans, but we've been meaning to ask."

"Oh, yeah. I passed through Marietta a few days ago and noticed a flyer in the coffee shop. We'd love to come."

"Great."

He paused, as though waiting for her to say something else. Then he finally spoke, breaking the awkward silence. "Thank you for the invitation. Is there something else I can do for you?"

He paused again, then before it could get uncomfortable, went on. "If that's all..."

"Actually, Charles. There's something else..."

"Not another mystery?" His tone sounded amused but hesitant. Not that Tess could really blame him. He'd helped out with two others, but she was sure he didn't appreciate three amateur sleuths doing law enforcement's job.

"Sort of. We've come across a situation here. But I can't give you any details just yet."

"Okay, then I'm not sure how I can help."

"The FBI handles missing person cases, right?"

"Is someone missing? You ladies are okay?"

"Oh, yes. Of course, we're fine. It's just that...We were wondering if you can recall whether or not there was a missing person case with maybe a sizable sum of money involved somewhere around Thanksgiving, or probably a week after."

"Tess, why are you asking?"

"I promise I'll fill you in if you know of a missing person around the end of November." She tapped her desk. "Like I said, it would have to be one where a large amount of money was involved."

"But there's nothing concrete for you to go on other than a hunch?"

"A hypothesis," Tess replied. "And you know, a hypothesis needs to be tested. That's where you come in. Do you recall anything you can share with me?"

She heard him expel a heavy breath. "There's nothing off the top of my head that rings a bell. Certainly not one of my cases. But I'll tell you what. I'll look into it when I have a few minutes, and I'll call you back as soon as possible. Okay?"

Tess hung up feeling a little embarrassed that she'd ever brought up the idea of Titus being FBI. If she hadn't become acquainted with Charles, she likely would never have even considered such an idea. Well, there was nothing she could really do about it now.

Karl and Shyla were coming from the café when she left the office. They were the last customers to be served lunch, so Taylor and Robin were cleaning up around them when Tess left a few minutes earlier.

"How'd the interview go?" She smiled at the hand-holding couple.

"It was... fine," Shyla said. She glanced at Karl, who didn't seem very optimistic either.

"Was there a problem?"

"She's as crazy as a bat," Karl said with a slight grin. "Other than that, no problem at all."

"I should've warned you. Molly's mind tends to wander at times."

"Oh, does it?" His grin turned into a self-deprecating laugh. "She thought I was an idiot for not being able to follow her trails. She did talk about Figgy in New York and her being married to an awful man. Then she started talking about Al Capone. And the only one that was ever allowed to take care of him was Mickey."

Tess's lips twitched with amusement. "Mickey? Do you remember a Mickey in the stories about Al Capone?"

Karl's frustration was nearly palpable as he shook his head. "It could be Mickey Mouse for all the sense she made."

"I think that's just her personality, with or without dementia. But I have heard from her grandson's wife, Willa, that she's getting more and more forgetful of the present and frequently slides into her past."

The elevator dinged, pulling Tess's gaze for a split second. She smiled as Titus approached. "Going out for the day?"

"Physical therapy awaits."

"Do you want me to call you a cab?"

"We're going out," Shyla said. "Can we drop you somewhere?" She stepped toward him and held out her hand. "I don't think we've officially met. I'm Shyla Mannus. This is my husband, Karl."

"Titus Jones." Titus accepted a handshake from each. "Thank you for offering, but I already called a cab. It should be here any second. It was nice to meet you both. I'll go wait on the porch, if you'll excuse me."

"It's going to be a lot of fun piecing together footage we can actually use," Karl said after Titus left.

"I take it you couldn't get her to talk about the mob?"

"Except for Capone." He shook his head. "Not any mobsters she could possibly have known. She would have been a really young girl when he went to prison. I thought for sure showing her the newspaper clipping I found would trigger something and get her talking." He sighed. "But there was nothing."

"Well," Tess said, "maybe there's nothing to uncover about the O'Haras. Just because her sister was married to an alleged mob boss doesn't mean Molly O'Hara and her husband were involved. Maybe that's why they moved to Marietta in the first place. To start their lives together away from that influence."

"That's true." Shyla took up the gauntlet. "After all, their son became a police officer, as well as their grandson, Johnny. And his son Justin is a firefighter. So they must have done something right."

Karl shrugged. "Maybe. Or maybe the O'Hara men went into public service to throw the police off the scent. Maybe they were just infiltrating the department to keep their family business safe."

Shyla nudged him. "Conspiracy theorist."

Karl leaned over and dropped a quick kiss on her lips, then glanced at Tess. "We're off. The Bickerton ladies have agreed to talk with me. It took me three days to get a meeting, so we don't want to be late."

"Be sure to go easy on them. Sometimes they talk a mile a minute. But other times, they keep a tight lid on their information. They have their reasons for sharing information or not."

"I'll be as gentle as if they were my grandmas."

Shyla winked at her. "And I'll make sure of it."

As Tess watched them walk toward the door, her mind went back to Tuesday during lunch, when Shyla sat in the café while the ladies shared their own theories about the O'Haras. She couldn't stop her grin. Clearly, Shyla was just as invested in this story as Karl. Who knew? Maybe it would work out the way the couple hoped, and the sisters would be chatty.

LuAnn and Janice stood together behind the counter. "Where are they going?" Janice asked as Tess approached.

"They have an interview with the Bickerton ladies. I guess Shyla's eavesdropping at lunch Tuesday paid off."

"Have either of you thought about what the ladies said about that Jack O'Hara?"

Tess nodded. "Do either of you remember reading anything about him?"

"Not me." LuAnn shook her head. "But it has me curious. Maybe sometime soon we can sit down while we're filling eggs and look through the journal. I'd say tonight, but after choir practice, I don't think I'll have the energy to do both."

Tess and LuAnn had joined the choir in preparation for the church's Easter cantata. "Good idea," Tess said. "Maybe we can solve one mystery—but it won't be before the birthday party, that's for sure."

LuAnn picked up a small notebook they wrote messages on and showed it to her. "Ed called a little while ago. Your car is ready, but he said he's taking off early today, so you can pick it up first thing tomorrow."

Relieved, Tess nodded. "I'll be glad to have wheels of my own again."

"One of us will take you after breakfast," Janice offered.

Tess smiled at her friends. It was wonderful to have people in her life she could count on.

CHAPTER EIGHT

Tess stood in the soprano section of the choir as Thursday night practice for the Easter cantata got underway. Janice sat the piano, where she'd reigned during the decades her husband was pastor of Christ Fellowship. LuAnn stood, shoulders straight and choir book in hand, at the front of the alto section. The practices had started a little slow, but they had improved so much that Tess was looking forward to standing with the choir on Easter morning to celebrate the resurrection of Jesus.

Margaret Ashworth, who ran the historical society, stood beside her for the next hour as a fellow soprano. When the practice broke up, they moved to the side of the platform. Tess decided to bring up the diary to see if Margaret remembered anything about a Jack O'Hara. "Margaret, how have things been?"

"About like usual." Margaret's face brightened, and Tess was struck with an uncomfortable twinge of guilt that she'd never reached out in friendship to Margaret. Except for cursory hellos and goodbyes when they met in public, she'd mostly only spoken to her when she and LuAnn and Janice had questions about the inn or the diary. And, truth be told, that was the only reason for a conversation now. She'd have to make up for her oversight later. For now, she stood quietly as Margaret answered Tess's question at length. "Oh, we've been doing well. The historical society is hopping with interest in the old days lately. I suppose Molly O'Hara's birthday has something to do with that." Her lips twitched in amusement. "That reporter from Channel 8 has been in several times this week—and his wife—she's a sweet woman. Have you met her?"

"Yes, they've been staying at the inn all week." Tess smiled as they turned and walked toward LuAnn and Janice. "It's their tenth anniversary."

"Oh, that's right. They did tell me they were staying with you. Hi, you two," she said to LuAnn and Janice. "I was just telling Tess that we've had extra visitors at the historical society the last week or so."

"Karl and Shyla have been there," Tess said with a sideways glance at her friends.

Janice laughed and focused her gaze on Margaret. "Karl is bound and determined to prove we've been living with a crime family in our midst for seventy years."

"Longer than that," Margaret said offhandedly as they walked together to the church doors. "He was looking for some evidence of a Jack O'Hara from way back during the Civil War." She frowned. "Have you all come across anything about him at the inn?"

Disappointment balled in Tess's stomach. If she was asking them about Jack O'Hara, then she must not remember anything about him.

LuAnn shook her head. "The Bickerton sisters mentioned him the other day, but we had never heard anything about him. Is there nothing at the historical society from old newspapers or town documents that might mention him?"

"Nothing I've ever seen. But then, I'd never heard the name until this week either, so I haven't looked."

Margaret stopped in front of her car. "I'd better get on home. You three want to catch lunch one day soon?"

"That sounds good, Margaret," Janice said. "Likely, it'll have to wait until we get through this Easter egg hunt at the inn though. It's turning into a real circus, with face painting and balloon animals and bouncy houses. The kids are going to love it, but goodness gracious goat, it's a lot of work."

Margaret nodded. "I saw Robin over at the barbeque place yesterday. She said you have six thousand plastic eggs to fill with candy and prizes. You all doing that by yourselves?"

Tess laughed. "For the most part. Robin and Taylor have pitched in here and there when they have a few extra minutes, and Winnie took a box of three hundred home, but she's not starting on them until after Molly O'Hara's party tomorrow."

"I think it's a good thing you're doing." Margaret's eyes narrowed. "It must be costing you a bundle. If you decide you need to sell any more of those antiques, you know I get first dibs on that silver tea service. Not that I'm coveting it—but I'd buy it for the right price."

Tess could feel Janice bristle at the mention of the antiques they'd received as an inheritance a few months ago. Margaret had been eyeing several of the pieces they'd kept at the inn. The silver tea service had especially been in her line of sight.

"We better be going," LuAnn said, looping her arm through Janice's.

"Nice talking to you all," Margaret said as she opened her car door. "I'll be calling you for that lunch once things settle down over there."

Tess waved. "We look forward to it."

They waited for her to fire up her car before they walked the next few car lengths to Janice's vehicle.

"Well, that's that," LuAnn said with a sigh as she climbed into the back seat. "She doesn't know any more about this elusive Jack O'Hara than we do."

Janice started the car and waited for everyone to buckle up. "If anyone has ever heard of Jack O'Hara—besides Irene and Thelma, of course—it would've probably been Margaret."

Tess clicked her seat belt and sat straight in her seat. "Maybelline Rector might know something about it." The curator of the Underground Railroad Museum knew more about the inn and Prudence Willard's involvement in the Underground Railroad than anyone they knew. More than that, she had what seemed like a personal mission to maintain the town's historical feel.

They drove through town, and just as they passed Jeremiah's Coffee House, a familiar figure caught Tess's attention. "Hey, look. Is that Titus?" He was standing by the door, speaking to a dark-haired woman. Her hands were on her hips, and her upper body leaned toward him as though they were having heated words.

Slowing the car to a crawl, Janice peered closer. "It is! Who is that woman with him?"

"I've never seen her," LuAnn said. "Do they look like they're arguing?"

"Sort of," Tess said.

"Should I stop?" Janice asked. "We could get a cup of tea."

Tess observed the pair in the light of the coffee shop. "Don't you think that would be a little too obvious?"

"Not to mention intrusive," LuAnn said.

"Titus wouldn't have to know we were curious," Janice said, but pushed on the gas and drove by. "He probably would've thought we were just getting tea, which we would be."

"Oh well. It's likely he just met her while he was getting coffee, and they were leaving at the same time." Still, Tess felt a twinge of curiosity herself.

Janice shook her head as she pulled into the parking lot. "The conversation seemed a little intense for a chance meeting."

"Maybe. But I'm no body language expert."

"Do you think he was meeting her last night?" LuAnn asked. "When we were walking Huck?"

They parked and walked together to the inn. "I guess that's possible. But that doesn't have to mean something mysterious." Tess dropped her tone as they stepped inside. "Maybe he met her over the past four months, and they're dating."

Janice kept her voice low. "She looks a little young."

Tess glanced around the inn. It was just after eight, and everything seemed quiet. Of course, they only had three rooms full tonight, and those included Titus and the Mannuses. "Maybe it's a May-December thing."

"Now we're just gossiping," LuAnn said. "I'm going to check on Huck. You guys coming?"

Tess gave a sigh. "I suppose it wouldn't hurt to fill up a few dozen plastic eggs before bedtime."

The front door opened just as they reached the steps. They turned to find Titus walking into the foyer. "Evening, ladies." His smile seemed weary and didn't quite reach all the way to his eyes, and he leaned more heavily on his cane than usual.

"We just got back from choir practice," Janice said. "Are you going up this way?"

He eyed the stairs, then shook his head. "If you don't mind, I'm going to take the elevator."

"Of course, Titus," LuAnn said. "We'll see you for breakfast."

They turned to walk up the steps and checked on each floor as they did so. Everything was quiet. As they reached their fourth-floor apartments, Janice waited while Tess unlocked the door. "He certainly doesn't look like a man in love, does he?"

Stepping inside, they closed the door. Tess shook her head. "I don't think so."

Maybe Janice was right, and the woman they'd seen him with did present another mystery to be solved. But short of nosiness, she didn't see how they could draw him into that conversation.

"Grab the eggs," Janice said.

LuAnn came into the room behind a prancing Huck who stopped and said a doggie hello to both Tess and Janice, then went straight for the door. "I'll be back to help fill those as soon as Huck is done." LuAnn glanced at the bags strewn across the sitting area they shared. "How many more do we have to fill?"

Tess grinned at her. "Don't even think about that. Think about all the ones we've already filled."

"I'll be back."

"Lock up when you come back, will you? Everyone seems to be in for the night."

Janice reached for a bag of eggs and a handful of candy. "There's nothing sweeter than watching chubby little hands reaching for hidden eggs. Unless it's the smiles on their faces when they hold them up and show their mommies and daddies. Trust me," she said, "our efforts for the community children are more than worth it."

April 7, 1863

Prudence woke with a start before dawn. What was different? Then she remembered the boy, the dog…the map. She lay still, staring at the ceiling for a few minutes, allowing her heartbeat to return to a normal rhythm. There was no point trying to resume sleep, so she pushed aside the heavy quilt and slowly swung her feet around until they touched the cold floor.

Jason shifted in his sleep but didn't waken.

She silently counted to ten, just to be sure she hadn't disturbed her husband and stood, pulling the covers over him to hold in the warmth.

She lifted the lamp from the table next to their bed and grabbed her dressing gown, tiptoeing to the door. Once outside the bedroom with the door firmly closed behind her, she set the lamp on the table and wrapped the gown around herself. She hated to disturb their guest, but the tinderbox and matches were on the mantel. Jason had promised that if their crops yielded a profit this year he would buy her a bundle of sulfur matches to get them through the winter. He wouldn't hear of allowing her to spend her meager earnings from the Riverfront House, and, indeed, had hinted more than once of late that there was no longer need for the ruse of her working there in order to help escaping slaves, as there were none to help these days.

She stopped short as the tiny spark of a flame and glowing embers from last night's fire lit enough of the room to reveal that the child was not there.

As quickly as possible, she lit the lamp and walked to the door. It was ajar, and the hinges creaked as she pulled it open and stepped onto the porch. A low growl met her, and fear shot through her stomach. For a split second she expected to be torn apart by a half-starved dog. Gathering her courage, she raised the lamp. Relief flooded her.

Boy and dog huddled together for warmth. The animal didn't move but kept a watchful and wary eye on her. She set the lamp on the porch railing and stepped back inside, grabbed the blankets from the floor, and said a hasty prayer that the child's protector wouldn't tear her to pieces while she covered the boy.

He kept her in his sights but seemed to understand as she spoke softly and laid the blankets over the sleeping child. Seeing she posed no threat, the dog dismissed her with a quick sigh as he laid his head back down and closed his eyes.

She settled down for the next half hour, reading the Scriptures and communing with the Lord. By the time she began cooking breakfast, she had found a sense of peace that she hadn't even realized was missing.

She had just pulled a pan of fluffy, golden-brown biscuits from the oven when movement behind her caught her attention. She turned and froze. The boy stood there, accompanied by a large, imposing man. How on earth he had gotten by the dog, Prudence couldn't imagine, but Jack O'Hara, the newest member of their township, held the child by his collar. The terrified child silently pleaded for help.

"Jack. Kindly unhand that child. Come and sit at my table, and I will pour thee some coffee."

"This boy's mangy varmint went after one of my best laying hens a couple o' days ago." He released the child, who backed away until he bumped the wall, then slid down, making himself as small as possible.

"It must not have been much of a mouthful, the way he devoured half a ham yesterday, bone and all." She tried not to smile, but Jack O'Hara had been a trial to several families since he'd arrived just six months ago. He was certainly not of the Friends and made no attempt to join in on community days—religious or otherwise.

"I don't need you makin' fun, Mrs. Willard."

With a sigh, Prudence reached to the kitchen shelf and felt behind the bag of flour for the jar she'd hidden there. Thinking of the fabric and shoes she was planning to buy, she felt a sinking in her stomach. Nevertheless, the child had become her responsibility, and the faster she got rid of the troublesome neighbor, the better. "How much restitution does thee require for the hen, Jack?"

He dipped his head but not before Prudence noticed his face had darkened in color. Good! He should be ashamed of himself. "Mrs. Willard. The dog didn't catch my hen. He just…um tried. I scared him off with buckshot before he could do any damage."

"I see." She screwed the lid back on the jar. "And how did thee know they had taken refuge in my home?"

"I tracked them here."

With a sigh, she replaced the jar, grateful she wouldn't be obligated to pay out any of her wages today. "I fear the poor animal is starving." Prudence lifted the plates from the shelf and began setting five places. She motioned the terrified boy to the table. "My husband and I have taken the child and his dog under our wing, so we will keep him fed. Now that we have this matter settled, won't thee join us for breakfast?"

"You letting him sit at the table with you?"

Her eyebrows rose. "Of course. I admit he was layered in dirt when he arrived yesterday, but he's had a thorough scrubbing." She smiled, deliberately misunderstanding his insinuation that a boy with dark skin was unfit to sit at a white table. She almost laughed. If Jack O'Hara only knew her bloodline. She'd once been a slave. Jason had Melungeon blood as well. The fact that they were both light enough to pass for white had worked in their favor these past years as they served their Father in heaven by escorting many slaves on their journey to freedom. She would not apologize for the deception. If it displeased the Lord, she would address it when they met face-to-face.

"I am afraid I was forced to give away most of my ham to the aforementioned dog, but there are biscuits and eggs a-plenty, and thee is most welcome to share our breakfast."

Prudence continued setting the table as Jack seemed to be mulling the invitation over. Relief nearly overwhelmed her when he walked to the table, despite the muddy trail his boots left in his wake.

"I don't suppose it'll hurt anything. Thank you kindly, ma'am. And I hope you'll forgive me for busting in here like I did."

He ruffled the boy's hair and took a seat next to him. "I didn't mean any harm to the little fella. Looks like he might've needed the food more than I did." He gave a jovial laugh and rubbed his protruding belly to emphasize his words.

The bedroom door opened, and Jason made his appearance, fully dressed, but with his hair slightly mussed.

"Good morning, Husband." Prudence went to him and kissed his cheek. "We have a guest for breakfast. Thee remembers Jack O'Hara?"

CHAPTER NINE

The amount of activity at the inn, from the second their feet hit the floor the next morning, was tantamount to a frenzy as far as Tess was concerned. Not only did Winnie prepare a wonderful breakfast for their guests and customers, she was busy with prep work for the food for Molly O'Hara's birthday party that night.

By midafternoon, the lunch crowd had come and gone, and Winnie, along with the two college-age helpers she'd hired, loaded up and headed toward the O'Hara house to begin setting up for the party.

With Robin manning the front desk, the three Inn Crowd ladies piled into Janice's car to go pick up Tess's car from Ed Baxter's shop. But there was no sign of anyone when they arrived. And the doors were locked. "He must have closed up early today," Tess said, disappointed that she'd likely have to wait until Monday to get her car.

Janice shook her head. "It would've been nice if he'd called. He's the one who said you could pick it up today."

"Well," LuAnn said. "He did say first thing this morning."

Tess shrugged. "At least my two best friends will give me a ride when I'm in a pinch."

Close to home, they stopped at a red light, and Janice gave a deep huff of a breath.

"What is it, Janice?" Tess asked from the back seat. "You okay?"

Instead of answering, Janice whipped the car into an illegal U-turn, barely missing a blue Subaru and a lamppost, and headed back down the street.

"What on earth are you doing?" LuAnn pressed a fist to her chest. "You about gave me a heart attack."

"I think if anyone knows about Jack O'Hara, it's got to be Maybelline. You said it yourself last night."

Tess had grabbed the back of LuAnn's seat during the Indy 500 move Janice had just made, and her own heart rate hadn't returned to normal. But Janice did have a point. "You know how cagey Maybelline can be. So we can't go in there guns a-blazing. Remember we have to stay calm and ask the right questions. And for goodness' sake, Janice, warn us next time you plan a move like that."

"Should we take the time to stop?" LuAnn asked. "Winnie probably needs our help."

"She's got those two college kids helping her. We can take a few minutes to try to solve this Jack O'Hara thing."

They walked into the Marietta Underground Railroad Museum minutes later, having fully recovered from the near accident. Tess was always filled with just a little sadness walking through the museum that showed what life was like for the slaves. LuAnn exhaled softly as she stood in front of a shadowbox and stared at a token minted in 1838 and sold by abolitionist women to raise money and bring awareness to their cause. A slave woman on her knees in chains was etched into the token, and the words "Am I not a woman and a sister?" was inscribed on it. "This one gets to me every time I see it," she said.

The office door was half open, and Tess could see there was someone inside. "Hello?" she called out.

A second later a rail-thin woman appeared in the doorway. Her burnt-orange hair was a stark contrast to her pale skin. "Oh, it's you three."

Janice's heels clicked on the floor as she walked toward her. "We have a couple of questions for you."

"Again? Do you have an appointment?"

"No," LuAnn said, with a sweeping wave at the empty room. "And it doesn't look like we need one today." She softened the words with a smile. "This place is such a treasure trove. Your love of preserving history shines in every display."

Maybelline pursed her coral-painted lips, but her expression softened from irritation to resignation. "You might as well come on in. And thank you for the compliment, LuAnn, if you really mean it."

Tess glanced at LuAnn. Her face was flushed, and Tess figured Maybelline's suspicion was at least partly right. While they did admire her detail for history, they also needed Maybelline's edges to be a little less sharp today so she would answer their questions without the usual song and dance.

Pulling a chair from the corner of the room, Tess sat beside Janice with LuAnn in the chair on the other side. Maybelline sat behind the ornate desk and leaned back in her chair, folding her arms across her chest. "What is it you ladies want this time? I know it's not my company you're after."

"We may as well just come to the point," Tess said. "What do you know about a man named Jack O'Hara? He would have lived in Marietta during the Civil War, and likely knew Prudence and Jason Willard, if our information is right."

Maybelline wrote something on a paper in front of her. "Where did you hear that name?"

LuAnn leaned forward. "The Bickerton sisters. They had lunch at the inn a few days ago and mentioned the first O'Hara—a man named Jack—lived here during the Civil War."

Maybelline gave a nonchalant wave. "You know those ladies aren't firing on all cylinders."

"Oh, I don't know." Tess sat up straighter. "It's true their bodies might be getting a little frail, but their minds are as sharp as can be. They remember a lot." She narrowed her gaze and looked Maybelline dead in the eye. "So, have you ever heard of him?"

Maybelline shifted her gaze between them. "What if I have? What makes you think I know any more than the Bickerton ladies already told you?"

This is where they had to tread lightly with Maybelline. The past had taught them she wasn't exactly a fountain of free-flowing information. Tess put a hand on the dark finish of the polished-to-a-shine desktop. "The Bickertons told us Jack O'Hara is mentioned in Prudence Willard's diary."

Maybelline gave a short laugh that bordered on bitter. "Why are you asking me? You have copies. Why don't you just look it up?"

This wasn't going to be easy. Janice shifted forward a little, so Tess ceded the floor to her. While they all tried to keep their conversation full of grace on a regular basis, Janice seemed to succeed the most often with difficult people. "We haven't had the time yet to do that, and we knew that you would be the one to ask and maybe give us a clue what date to look under."

"Please don't patronize me, Janice. I know everyone thinks I'm a big joke in this town. But all I want to do is preserve and protect our history. Someday, when Marietta is nothing more than chain stores and strip malls, maybe then my efforts will be appreciated."

"Maybelline," LuAnn said, her tone pitched a little higher than normal in surprise, "of course, we appreciate your efforts." Her voice filled with a little more gentleness than usual. "That's why we came to you."

The proud woman seemed to realize she had allowed the cracks in her wall to show, and she stood abruptly. "I don't remember any Jack O'Hara in the journal, but I'll keep an eye out, and if I come across any documents or old photos of him, I'll let you know. You all know the way out."

Apparently dismissed, Tess stood slowly, as did Janice and LuAnn. "Thank you for your time," Tess said.

With a sharp nod, Maybelline acknowledged their thanks, then sat back down in her chair and rummaged through a stack of papers as though they weren't still in the office.

Tess shrugged and motioned to the door with a jerk of her thumb. They walked silently back through the front room of the museum and into the cool spring air.

"Well," Janice said. "That's that." She unlocked the car doors with the remote a few feet before they reached the car.

When they were inside and buckled, LuAnn spoke up. "There's nothing for it, ladies. We're just going to have to find the time to comb through Prudence's journal and find Jack."

⁂

Molly O'Hara's birthday party was already in full swing by the time Tess, Janice, and Titus arrived five minutes before seven, the time specified on the invitation.

"Winnie must be beside herself," Janice whispered as they looked around at the packed-out mansion. "Do you think she made enough food?"

Tess shrugged. "Should we find her and offer to help?"

Backing away, Janice held up her hands in defense. "She's already threatened to quit the inn if we even try it. She said it would make her look incompetent."

"Well then, we should go give our regards to our hostess."

Willa O'Hara, wife of Sergeant Johnny O'Hara, met them just as they reached the accent table close to the door and set down the birthday card they'd brought. In lieu of actual gifts, the invitation suggested a donation to buy Easter meals and baskets for needy families.

"Lovely night for a party, Willa," Janice said.

"Finally, someone I actually invited." She waved her fingers and shook her head nervously. "Oh, this party. I wish we'd just taken Gigi to dinner instead." In contrast to her usually calm, cool, and collected demeanor, Willa clearly was about to completely unravel like a fifty-year-old rag rug.

"Take a deep breath, Willa," Tess said evenly, trying to keep her from having a full-blown breakdown. "Can we do something to help?"

Willa shook her head and leaned in, dropping her voice. "We're already at capacity. Justin says if we squeeze any more people into this house, he'll shut the whole thing down."

"He's just looking out for your safety."

Justin O'Hara took his job as a firefighter and town protector very seriously. Apparently, he wasn't going to bend the rules, even for his own great-grandmother and mother.

Willa's face relaxed a little as she allowed a tiny smile. "I think he was just showing off for Saffron, but why on earth do people think they can just crash a party like this?"

There was security at the doors, and each person had to show his or her invitation, so Tess had no idea why Willa was in such a state. "Are you letting in people without invitations, or are they hopping the wall in their formal attire?"

"That's just something I can't figure out, Tess." Willa shook her head. "Everyone here has shown an invitation. I sent out thirty-five, and even at that, I assumed only about thirty would come, and most of those would bring a guest. For the life of me, I can't imagine how this happened. I started getting RSVP emails from people I know I didn't invite. People must have made their own invitations."

Fake birthday party invitations for an elderly woman? Tess was hard-pressed to hold back a grin. But in her present state,

Willa would never see the humor. And of course Tess couldn't blame her. "I suppose everybody and their brother wanted to come to this shindig. It's the place to be tonight. I'm not surprised they're crashing. Did you use an event planner? We are using Kay Ingram for our Easter event at the inn next Saturday. She's saved us a lot of headaches."

"Sure she has, for something big like that. But I only planned for about sixty people." Willa sounded incredulous. "That's no more than a holiday dinner at our house between the O'Haras and my side of the family. This is turning into a circus. In her mind, Gigi is back in the nineteen sixties and thinks she's hosting John F. Kennedy's victory party. And with a reporter here too. All I can be grateful for is that I hired your Winnie and not some incompetent fool to do the catering. Just yesterday, I told her to plan for at least a hundred people, and here she's got enough food laid out to feed a football stadium full of hungry fans. Which we apparently have."

"Winnie is the best. She's going to make all this go smooth as *buttah*," Janice said. "Did Johnny's mother make it to town for the party?"

Willa shook her head. "Johnny's brother didn't either. He called to tell Johnny their mom is in the hospital with pneumonia, poor thing."

"That's too bad," Tess said.

"Yes, this is her third bout with it in two years," Willa said. Then she brightened. "How are your plans for the Easter egg hunt coming along? Or EGGstravaganza, as I saw in the paper you're calling it." She smiled and seemed to relax a bit as she focused on something besides the birthday debacle.

"We're getting our ducks in a row," Janice said. "For a while I was afraid it was going to be all a bunch of chaos like..."

Tess tensed and glanced at Willa, hoping Janice's slip of the tongue didn't upset her. Instead, Willa laughed. "Like this? Be glad you have that event planner. Sometimes the best-laid plans get all unraveled."

"Actually," Tess said, "we were hoping to ask the fire chief if he would park a fire truck at the inn during the egg hunt so the children could see what one looks like up close."

"I'm sure he wouldn't mind. He's done it for other community events. I'll ask Justin to run it by him."

"Thank you. We appreciate it." Tess placed her hand on Titus's arm. "Let us introduce you to Titus Jones."

Titus smiled at Willa. "I don't generally take up a lot of room, nor am I inclined to eat much at parties. At least not that I know of."

A gracious answering smile instantly curved Willa's mouth, and she turned her full attention, or so it seemed, to Titus. "Of course, Titus, you are absolutely welcome."

Titus held out his hand, which Willa took. "Nice to meet you, Mrs. O'Hara."

"Please, it's Willa. When people around here say 'Mrs. O'Hara' they're typically referring to Molly."

"Titus is staying at the inn all month," Tess told her.

"How nice. And where are you from?" She frowned. "You look familiar. Do we know each other?"

Tess's senses alerted, and she looked askance at Titus to see if there was any reaction. An awkward silence hung in the air as they waited for his answer. "I don't think we've met."

"Oh," Willa said. "Maybe you just have a familiar face."

"That's possible." He cleared his throat and shifted, wincing as he put weight on his injured leg.

Janice broke the awkwardness. "Oh, goodness gracious goat."

"What now?" Willa asked, not turning. "I can't look."

"I think Molly just threw a canapé at Karl Mannus."

The well-timed distraction couldn't have been more welcome.

Willa laughed and raised her perfectly arched eyebrows. "She's not too keen on reporters. And this one has been hanging around all week. I'd best go and tend to the situation."

Janice grinned after their hostess walked away. "I think I'll take my life into my own hands and try to get Winnie to let me help. I'm pretty sure even her very well organized whiteboard isn't going to salvage this overgrown party. Thank goodness it wasn't a sit-down dinner."

Tess took Titus's arm and introduced him to a few people from town. She had just started to head for Pastor Ben Murphey and his wife, Paige, when she noticed they were chatting with Ed Baxter and Dane. She needed to talk to Ed about her car, but she wasn't sure if they would bring up the money in the suitcase or not, and she didn't want Titus to feel uncomfortable. "Wait."

"Something wrong?" Titus asked. "We could try to find a place to sit, although with so many people, I'm not sure—"

"Nothing's wrong. Let's just..." She glanced around until her gaze caught the French doors. "You haven't seen the garden yet. Let's get some air."

"It is a little stuffy."

They were almost to the doors when Molly called from across the room. "Hey! Hey, you two. Wait."

Titus glanced over his shoulder. "I think she means us."

Tess turned, matching Titus's movements. The woman of the hour herself. Ninety-five-year-old Molly O'Hara, her hair dyed the same brassy red it had always been. Her crooked fingers no longer bore jeweled rings, but her wrists made up for it in flashy diamonds and emeralds. A sparkling emerald and diamond tiara capped off her look. Tess was surprised to see that around her neck, in contrast to her bling, Molly wore what looked to be a large filigreed antique locket.

The old lady's eyes flashed as she pointed her gold-handled walking stick straight at Titus. "You."

Titus's eyebrows went up, and he pointed at his chest. "Me, ma'am?"

"Don't you play stupid with me, mister. Where is my sister?"

Poor Titus stared, his mouth open as he tried to figure out how to answer.

"I haven't heard from Figgy in ages, and I want to know where she is."

The commotion was beginning to draw attention as those close by stopped their conversations and took steps closer to them.

Titus glanced at Tess for support just as she was about to step in anyway. "I—I couldn't really say. Maybe—"

"Molly, I think you have this man confused with someone else. Mr. Jones is a guest at Wayfarers Inn."

"Don't speak to me as if some of my marbles are missing, young lady. I think I know Mickey when I see him."

Tess saw Molly's great-grandson Justin O'Hara headed their way, decked out in his firefighter's dress uniform. "Everything okay, Gigi?"

The expression on her face shifted like magic, and in its place a bright smile lit up her eyes and stretched her thin lips. "Everything is just lovely, sweet boy."

"Let me help you back to your chair. There are a lot of people here who haven't had a chance to wish you happy birthday yet."

"Oh. Is it my birthday?"

"Yes, ma'am. It is. All these people are here to celebrate with you."

"Honey, that's so nice. Let's be sure they all have enough to eat. Are we going to play Pin the Tail on the Donkey? I don't much enjoy that game. I prefer musical chairs. Do you think Mama bought me the doll from New York?"

Her voice trailed off as Justin gently escorted her back to her throne in the center of the room, a rose and gold printed wing chair. Tess watched them go, and her gaze landed on Karl Mannus, who followed close behind Molly, with Shyla holding the TV camera. Had they caught the entire exchange between Titus and the old lady? Too late, she thought of what it might mean for Titus to be caught on camera.

"That was certainly odd."

Tess turned at the sound of Titus's introspective voice.

"I wouldn't read too much into it, Titus. You heard Willa say earlier that Molly thought the party was for John F. Kennedy to celebrate his election."

Reaching up, he held the back of his neck for a beat, and his gaze shifted to Molly as Justin fussed around her and her guests paid their respects. Tess caught her breath as the elderly woman seemed to come back to herself. She settled eyes on Titus.

Tess touched his arm. "Should we go look at the garden now?"

He nodded, pulling his attention from Molly back to Tess as she led the way.

As they stepped into the cool, clear night, Titus took in a deep breath of sweet air. Tess smiled. "It's beautiful, isn't it? And when they decorate it for events like this, it's like something out of a magazine."

Titus nodded, but his eyes still seemed troubled. Tess wished there was something she could say that might comfort him after the encounter he'd just had. He turned and met her gaze. "Is it possible she knows me?"

"Molly?" Tess didn't suppress her grin. "I wouldn't put much stock in that whole episode, Titus. Her sister passed away last year around... Thanksgiving." She hesitated, swallowing hard past the sudden thought that lodged in her throat just short of her blurting it out. The timing of Titus's accident coincided with Figgy Kelly's death.

Catching movement to the side, Tess turned her head, and a shudder rolled up her spine. Karl stood a few feet away, staring, but not at her. His eyes were fixed firmly on Titus. Clearly, Titus was now on his radar. Karl's instincts were too well honed not to know there was some sort of story here. Not even the smell of roses and lilacs and the beauty of the garden could shake Tess's troubled thoughts.

CHAPTER TEN

The party celebrating the woman who had lived nine and a half decades didn't end until ten o'clock. Poor Willa rushed around the hired helpers, apologizing profusely, helping where she could, though Winnie grumbled that the woman got on her nerves and in the way. Brad Grimes offered to drive Titus back to the inn, and the men left right after the last of the guests filtered out, leaving a mess that would rival the day after a frat party. Over Winnie's objections, LuAnn, Janice, and Tess insisted on helping Winnie and her helpers with cleanup duty.

"You all are guests of this party," Winnie fussed. "You shouldn't be getting your hands—or your dress clothes—dirty. I signed up for this, you didn't."

LuAnn gave her the quickest, tightest hug Winnie would allow. "All for one, one for all."

"It's up to you, but I insist on paying you a fair wage for your time."

The three women looked at each other, at first in shock, then a sudden burst of laughter rose up between them.

"Oh, Winnie," LuAnn said. Winnie stepped back as it appeared she was going to have to stop working for another impulsive hug. "You aren't giving us a cent. Your fabulous meals are what make us a bed-and-breakfast. Without you, we'd just be a 'bed.'"

"Hogwash. Your blueberry muffins make mine taste like a stale box mix." But Winnie looked pleased at the compliment. Largely, Tess assumed, because their cook's blueberry muffins had actually been featured on a website that bore several celebrity recipes.

Janice laughed as she scrubbed a tray at the sink. "That's funny. 'A bed.'"

Her friend's belated laugh over LuAnn's comment brought a smile to Tess's lips, and she noted a grin on Lana's face as well. They definitely needed to help get this finished up so they could get Winnie home to bed after the long day.

With several women already working in the kitchen, Tess grabbed a silver tray and began to gather used plates and glassware from the main rooms. As she worked, her thoughts took her back to the conversations of the evening. It would be good to sit with LuAnn and Janice later and discuss Titus's encounter with that woman in Jeremiah's the night before. Not to mention what had happened between him and Molly earlier tonight.

A smile touched her lips as she gathered a stack of clear plastic hors d'oeuvres plates onto her tray. A loud snort caught her attention, and she looked around. "Willa!" a voice called out. Tess walked around a chair and found Molly blinking. A confused frown creased her brow.

"Can I help you, Mrs. O'Hara?" Tess asked.

The woman's eyes sharpened as she sat herself up a little higher. "Why did they leave me sleeping in this confounded chair? My neck's got a crick in it."

"I'm not sure. Should I find Willa for you?"

"What for?" She raised her walking stick and pointed to a large ottoman in front of her wing chair. "Sit down there and talk to me. No one ever talks to me." She heaved a long sigh. "They think I don't know they're all just waiting for me to die so they can have my money."

"Oh, I'm sure that's not true, ma'am."

Mrs. O'Hara snorted. "What do you know about it? They've been waiting ever since my sister passed last year." Another frown crinkled her brow. "Now, listen, what were you doing with Mickey earlier?"

"Mickey? I don't know anyone by that name."

"That's right. You called him something else, didn't you? Jones?"

Tess's heart rate sped up. "I did introduce you to a man earlier. Titus Jones. He's a guest at the inn."

"He took care of Capone, you know." She sighed and shook her head. "My sister loved him more than she loved her kids."

Clearly, she was regressing again. Did she suddenly think Titus was Elliot Ness, the FBI agent who "took care" of Al Capone? Of course, logically, Molly and her sister would have been children when Capone was arrested, so this line of conversation had to be pure fantasy. But it did make her wonder whether or not the rumors surrounding the O'Haras had any merit. Were they affiliated with the mob after all?

Before Molly could weave more of the tale her mind was telling her, Willa breezed in. "Oh, Gigi, you're awake."

"Yes, and I have a crick in my neck, thanks to you leaving me to sleep all cockeyed."

"I'm sorry. But you were sleeping so peacefully, we thought it best to let you rest. It was quite an exciting evening for you." Willa reached for the elderly woman who, surprisingly, allowed herself to be helped to her feet.

Up to her full height, which was no more than five feet, Mrs. O'Hara turned to Tess. "Tell Mickey to come around and see me soon. I want to hear all about how Capone is doing without my sister's coddling." She patted Willa's arm. "I better get up to bed. I'm so tired."

Willa turned to Tess. "Thank you for keeping her company. I don't want to keep you."

"My pleasure." Tess rose and grabbed the tray she'd set down on the table beside her. The room was nearly picked up.

"Don't worry about that, Tess. I've hired a cleaning crew to come in tomorrow."

"I don't mind one bit helping out. But if that's the case, I'll go back and help finish up in the kitchen."

"Tess? The guest you brought tonight does seem familiar. It could just be that I've seen him around town. But what do you ladies know about him?"

"Not a lot, to be honest. But no less than we usually know about our guests at the inn."

Molly gave an impatient huff, and Willa turned her attention back to her, leading her forward toward the stair lift.

Thirty minutes later, Tess, Janice, and LuAnn pulled into the parking area in front of the inn. Tess had told them the story of Molly's confusion about Titus.

As they walked toward the inn, they rehashed the evening.

"So," Janice said, "do you think Molly is confused, or does she really know Titus?"

"And Al Capone?" Tess said wryly.

"No, I guess you're right." Janice paused a second. "But Willa said he seems familiar to her too."

"But she admits that could just be from seeing him around town."

"True."

They walked into a quiet, dimly lit inn. After a quick walk-through to make sure everything was as it should be, they headed for the stairs.

Tess had planned to bring up the woman Titus met in the coffeehouse, but when they reached their apartment, Huck needed a walk. Janice accompanied LuAnn as she accommodated the dog while Tess took her weary body into her own suite and changed into her night clothes. She had already fallen into bed by the time she heard the front door open.

The look of certainty on Molly's face when she confronted Titus replayed in Tess's mind, impeding her sleep. Of course, it wasn't possible that he'd taken care of Al Capone, but her second insistence that she knew Titus made Tess wonder.

Titus's reaction had been one of bewildered amusement that seemed genuine. On the other hand, who was the woman who had confronted him in Jeremiah's? If Titus was Mickey, and there was a connection between him and Molly's sister, Figgy, there might be a lot more to Karl's mob theory than they had given him credit for.

After the late night and restless sleep, Tess practically dragged herself out of bed the next morning. She took a quick shower, fixed her bed, and headed down the dimly lit stairs. It was her Saturday to start baking the pastries that Winnie always prepared ahead for her days off, and cut up fruit for their guests. That also meant Tess started the coffee. That was why she frowned as she neared the kitchen and was confronted with the aromas of freshly brewed coffee and baking.

When she pushed open the kitchen door, she found LuAnn inside leaning against the counter with a steaming mug in her hand. She hadn't bothered lighting up the place, so only the soft glow above the sink offered any light. "Lu? What are you doing? You had breakfast prep last week."

"Couldn't sleep." She carried her coffee to the table and sat. "I haven't been up that long."

"Why couldn't you sleep? Too much adrenaline from the party?"

She shook her head. "It was Huck. He must have missed us last night. He wanted attention and needed out again."

"Oh? I didn't see him when I came down."

LuAnn smiled and took a sip of coffee. "That's because he went back to sleep as soon as he hopped in my bed. I finally decided to get a jump on breakfast for the guests."

Tess went straight to the cabinet and pulled out her favorite mug. She filled it just as the timer on the oven began to beep a one-minute warning. "Looks like the first batch of muffins is about done. What kind are they today?"

"Banana with cranberries. How did Titus enjoy the party? Other than that awkward scene Molly made."

Tess set her mug on the counter, then opened the oven and pulled out two pans of muffins, setting them on the cooling racks. Grabbing one of the pans of blueberry and lemon scones that were already prepared on the counter, she slid it into the oven, then the other, and reset the timer. She picked up her coffee and joined LuAnn at the table.

"He seemed to enjoy it, but Molly rattled him a little, I think." Tess had noticed him glancing at Molly several times with a pensiveness she could only assume meant he was troubled, or at least curious, about the conversation they'd had earlier. Especially considering the woman they'd seen him talking to outside the coffee house.

"Last night you acted as though Molly was just confused about him. What do you think now that you've slept on it?"

LuAnn knew her too well. "Who knows? There were so many people there, I was a little confused myself."

LuAnn chuckled. "Poor Willa. Evidently a lot of people didn't let a little thing like not having been invited keep them from the party of the year. Still, that's what happens when you insist on being rich and mysterious in a town full of curious people."

"I'd say poor Winnie more than poor Willa. She's the one who had to scramble to make sure the food stretched. I don't know how she did it." Tess sipped her coffee, letting the warmth bathe her throat. "I'm pretty sure we're never going to know the answer to that question. And I do think it turned out okay, all things considered."

"I suppose it turned out for Willa," LuAnn said. "But I'm not sure Titus would agree."

"Because of Molly confronting him?"

LuAnn nodded. "That, and the fact that Shyla filmed the whole thing. Unless I miss my guess, Karl is going to be following the scent."

"Maybe we should have thought things through before taking Titus with us to the party," Tess said. "I never even considered that something like that might happen though. Do you think we should have a talk with Karl? Appeal to his sense of reason? Or maybe even tell him about Titus having amnesia?"

"He may already know."

Alarm seized Tess, and she jumped as the oven timer beeped. "Why do you think that?"

"I saw him talking to Ed and Dane last night."

"He did interview the guests about Molly's birthday for his story."

"Yes, but they kept looking at Titus as they were talking." LuAnn stood and refilled her coffee, then poured what was left into a carafe. While she started a fresh pot, Tess pulled the scones out of the oven.

"The police told them about Titus having amnesia." LuAnn pulled a carton of coffee creamer from the refrigerator as she spoke. "And you confirmed that he was staying here at the inn when you took your car in to be looked at."

Tess grimaced at the realization that she had broken a cardinal rule by revealing a confidential detail about a guest. "You're right, I did." She carefully pulled two pans of breakfast casserole from the refrigerator. She glanced at the clock. Breakfast would start in an hour, just long enough for a casserole to cook. She carefully set one pan in the oven, leaving the other to go in the oven in a half hour so it would be fresher for their later guests. She set the timer and moved back to the table as Janice came into the kitchen. She was fully dressed and looked like she'd slept ten hours.

"Morning!" She noted the carafe on the table. "Is that still hot?"

"Yes, I just brought it over so I could start more to fill the thermal pots in the café."

Taking down three plates, Janice glanced over her shoulder. "Scones or muffins?" she asked, grabbing a cup by the handle. "So that was some party last night."

LuAnn decided on a muffin. "We were just talking about that party. I'm pretty sure Karl knows about Titus's amnesia. He was talking to Ed and Dane at the party, and they were looking at Titus."

Janice sighed. "It was bound to get out, I suppose."

Tess broke off a piece of a scone. "It probably never occurred to Ed to keep it a secret. Not to mention, Karl is a pretty skilled interviewer. He's good at getting information out of people and making them think they offered it on their own. We've seen that on TV, and even experienced it ourselves." She grinned at Janice, then popped the bite into her mouth and washed it down with coffee.

Now that the three of them were alone, it was a good time to put their heads together. "LuAnn, I think it's time to update that notebook of yours and see where we stand." Tess finished her scone and brushed her fingers together to rid them of crumbs. "And very soon, we're going to have to take the time to find out what Prudence can tell us. Jack O'Hara might just be the key to all of this."

Roland and Claire Abbott were middle-aged empty-nesters who traveled between New York, where Claire was from and where they lived now, and Columbus, where Roland had grown up and where their son played football for Ohio State University. This was their fourth time staying at the inn, so they were familiar with the routine. Once they were settled, they came down for lunch just in time to get some soup before the café closed.

Tess was just loading the dishwasher when Taylor entered the kitchen. "The Abbotts want to know if you can come out and say hello." He walked to the sink where baking pans still waited to be washed. "I can finish up in here, if you'll keep an eye on their drinks."

"I'm pretty sure I get the better end of that deal," Tess said. "I accept."

Claire stood as Tess walked through the café toward them. "Tess, it's so good to see you!" She gave her a quick hug. "Will you join us?"

"I hate to interrupt your lunch."

"Not at all." Claire laughed. "We can eat and talk, can't we, Roland?"

Tess smiled and sat. "How have the two of you been?"

"Bored." Claire sighed. "I never really considered how lonely it would be once the kids moved out. With Heidi living on her own and her life so busy, we rarely see her. Even though she went to NYU and lives in Manhattan. And Josh is about to graduate from college."

"And probably getting married soon," Roland added.

"Married?" Tess lifted her eyebrows. "When did that happen?"

Claire rolled her eyes. "It hasn't yet. That we know of. We're having dinner with Josh tonight and meeting his girlfriend. He says they've been dating since last year."

Roland grinned. "That sounds like an announcement to me."

Karl and Shyla entered the café. Robin had informed them earlier that the couple had decided to stay through the weekend rather than check out today as they had originally planned.

"Did we miss lunch?" Shyla asked, disappointment edging her voice.

"Just barely," Tess said, smiling. "Let me go see what's left. Today we made chicken and vegetables with wild rice, or chili

132

in a bread bowl. Will either of those work if we're out of one or the other?"

"Either is fine with me," Karl said. "I'm starving."

Shyla nodded. "Me too. But don't go to extra trouble for us."

As luck would have it, Taylor had just turned off the fire under the pots, so both soups were still at health code temperatures. Tess prepared a bread bowl with chili and a bowl of the chicken and rice with a basket of yeast bread and delivered them while Taylor followed with colas for both and the pitcher of tea to refill the Abbots' drink glasses.

The two couples were sitting at the same table. The sight made Tess's heart swell. She loved to see strangers become friends. "I made a bowl of each," she said. "Who wants what?"

"Chili," Karl said the same time Shyla said, "Chicken and rice."

Their laughter brought the same from the Abbots and Tess.

"It's good to see you four are getting to know each other," Tess said.

Claire motioned toward Karl. "Karl tells us he's a TV anchor from Canton. We don't know any reporters."

"Well," Karl said amicably, "you do now."

"I suppose we do." Claire turned to Tess. "Will you pull up a chair and visit with us while we eat?"

Tess complied, making the four-top table into a little bit of a cramped five.

"Karl was telling us he's working on a story that he's hoping to submit in New York."

Karl met Tess's gaze. "It's a local New York station, not national, but it would be a start."

That explained why he was going after this mob story so hard. Karl was ready for a change.

"That's fantastic, Karl." Tess just hoped he wasn't planning to include Titus in his job-finding endeavor. "Channel 8 wouldn't be the same without you though."

He smiled with genuine pleasure—a smile that reached his eyes. "Thank you, Tess. It's nice to know I'd be missed."

"When does the story of Molly O'Hara's party air?"

"Oh, I have some voice-overs to do on Monday when I get back to the studio, then they'll edit and likely run it on Tuesday."

If the Abbotts hadn't been there, Tess would have asked him not to include any of the footage of Titus. She couldn't imagine why he would, but she didn't want to leave anything to chance. She made the mental note to speak with him later, when they had a minute alone.

Roland Abbott wiped his mouth with a napkin. "That must have been some party if it's making the news."

"Molly O'Hara turned ninety-five," Tess explained. "She's something of a matriarch in this area. She did a lot of charity work with underprivileged families in her day and marched for civil rights. I imagine if she'd been around back before the Civil War she'd have been working right alongside Prudence Willard saving runaway slaves right out of this very inn."

"I think so too, Tess." Shyla leaned forward, her blue eyes wide with excitement. "We also found out, during our interview, that she raised money for the families of soldiers who died in Korea and in Vietnam."

Karl cast a glance at Tess, then back to the Abbotts. "We also have evidence that ties the O'Haras directly to the Kelly family in New York."

"Oh? We know some Kellys, but they're not related to each other," Claire said. "One family we know has children who went to school with ours. They own a couple of restaurants that serve Irish beer. And the other Kellys..." She shook her head. "I can't think."

"You're thinking of Pat. He worked with me at the hospital years ago."

"Oh, that's right. The doctor."

"So," Karl said slowly. "Those are the only Kellys you know?"

Claire laughed. "Yes, except for the crime family. But thankfully, we don't know them—or more to the point, they don't know us."

Roland narrowed his gaze as he studied Karl's face. "You're saying this Molly O'Hara is linked to the syndicate Kelly family of New York City?"

Karl shrugged. "It seems that way."

Roland's lips twitched with amusement. "That's a little hard to believe. From New York all the way to a little town in Ohio?" He chuckled.

Karl's ears reddened, and Tess could see he was getting defensive. She couldn't really blame him. Shyla must have noticed the same thing. She reached out, and he calmed visibly at her touch. Still, in the end, he apparently needed the vindication. He reached into his leather bag and pulled out a folder. Opening it, he passed it to Roland. "It's dated 1965."

Tess moved slightly to get a better view of the photo from an old newspaper clipping. A young, beautiful Molly O'Hara stood next to a man who would definitely give any one of the Rat Pack a run for his money. Though the furnishings and décor were different than present day, the photo had definitely been taken at the O'Hara mansion, right there in Marietta. The O'Haras stood with another couple, the women in gorgeous cocktail gowns standing next to each other between the two men.

Karl pointed to the O'Haras. "That's obviously Molly and her late husband, Gibson."

Without her glasses, Tess couldn't read the small print even if she squinted. "The other two are…?"

He grinned. "The woman is Molly O'Hara's sister, Francine. They called her Figgy. But the other man, her husband, was the head of the Kelly family in New York. One of the last of the real Irish gangs before the crackdown by the police in the fifties. He lasted longer than most of the gangs, because, you know, all those Irish cops. They were either family or friends, and this guy wasn't a thug like the street guys. As you can see, he had finesse. My guess is he padded a lot of pockets to stay afloat as long as he did. They never did pin anything on him that stuck, but a lot of his underlings died in prison."

Roland held up his hands, palms up, as though surrendering. "I stand corrected." His eyes gleamed as he focused them on Karl. "Looks like you're going to be a great fit for our city."

While Tess was happy that Karl proved his point, she couldn't help but wonder how far he was willing to go to find his big story. And how would that tenacity affect Titus?

CHAPTER ELEVEN

May 10, 1863

Prudence praised the Lord that there was no reason to hurry the little boy to the next station along the journey to Canada. As a matter of fact, there was no real reason for him to go anywhere at all. Abraham Lincoln had set him free, and even though the Southern states did not recognize the president's authority to do so, they certainly were not going to bother chasing after a runaway child. She had not yet broached the topic with Jason, but what if the Lord had given them not a "package" to save, but a second child to love and raise?

It had been a little over a month since the Lord had handed the child over to them. And though he—and his dog—were still painfully thin, they no longer looked gaunt. But the boy still hadn't spoken a word. They called him Gideon, because any boy his age who had endured the amount of hardship he had, and all alone, surely had the heart of a warrior, despite appearances.

From the porch, the dog, whom Moses had fittingly named Brown, barked. Not the deep, growling, warning bark he'd used in the beginning before he realized Gideon was not in danger, but a bark of greeting.

Prudence cast a quick glance at Jason, and he rolled his eyes. "He has come again to eat our breakfast with us, I see."

"And as God has loved us, we will love our neighbor as ourselves. Doesn't thee agree, Husband?"

Jason gathered a slow breath and nodded as he exhaled. Prudence smiled to herself. After all, with two tender boys in the room, how else could he have responded? She inclined her head toward Gideon, who grinned and walked to the porch. Jack O'Hara had arrived for his daily breakfast with the family. Despite his initial hesitance to even sit at the table with Gideon, now it seemed as though he'd formed an attachment that defied explanation other than the hand of God Himself, for only God had the power to change a man's heart.

Prudence stood in the doorway waiting for Mr. O'Hara to dismount. His red face lit up at the sight of Gideon.

"Hello, lad!" he called out. "Come over here and get this bag of scraps I brought for your mutt. Now, no thanks needed. Roarke burned the beef anyway. It was either bury it or give it to the dog."

Gideon no longer walked with a head-down shuffle. The strength and confidence he had gained was nothing short of a miracle. He took the bag in one hand and the reins of Jack's horse in the other as the Irishman dismounted. Brown approached Jack, tentatively at first, then with a nudge against Jack's leg as the man reached out and scratched the dog behind his floppy ears. Gideon wrapped the reins around the post in front of the house and then offered Brown his treat.

"It is a pleasure to see thee, Jack. Thee will join us for breakfast?"

"Don't mind if I do." He grinned, turning to Gideon. "Lad, if it's all the same to you, go reach into my saddlebag and pull out the package that's inside."

Curiosity shone in the boy's eyes as he did as he was told.

"That's it," Jack said. "Give it to the missus."

With a frown Prudence took a package wrapped in brown paper and tied with a string.

"That there's a couple o' pounds of bacon from my smoke-house. Figured it was the least I could do with you inviting me to breakfast four times this week."

"Why, that wasn't necessary, Jack. It is our pleasure to have thee."

He glanced at the ground and shuffled his feet. Prudence's heart softened toward the man at his obvious discomfort. And she felt ashamed. The loud, often gruff neighbor had never been a favorite of those in the community. He was given to bouts of drunkenness and refused to attend any services, Quaker or otherwise. Prudence had seen his wife only a few times while at the mercantile, but had never even attempted to befriend her. Well, that was about to end.

As she poured their guest a cup of coffee and set plates of ham, eggs, and flapjacks, she broached the subject. "Jack, it would be our honor if thee and thy wife would join us for Moses's birthday dinner the day after tomorrow."

Reaching out, he grabbed two slices of ham with his fingers, and set them on his plate. "Ain't no Mrs. O'Hara. Just my spinster sister. She don't leave the farm much these days."

"Oh?" The news surprised Prudence. She had just assumed the woman was his wife. "Perhaps I will drop by for a visit."

"No, ma'am. She's not much a one for passin' the time o' day."

Stung, Prudence nodded. "I understand. I didn't mean to impose."

He scooped up three fried eggs, slapped them together with some ham between the two flapjacks, and lifted the whole concoction to his mouth.

Prudence forced herself not to stare, but when Gideon followed the older man's lead, it was more than she could stomach. She reached out and touched the boy's arm. When he glanced up, she shook her head and motioned to his plate and then his fork.

His expression fell in disappointment, but he understood and obeyed. Moses had been watching wide-eyed, and Jason's lips twitched in amusement.

When they finished breakfast, Prudence wrapped up the leftover ham and flapjacks and handed them to Jack. He took the package with only the smallest amount of embarrassment. "Mr. Willard," he said, his eyes fixed keenly on Jason, "I wonder if you'd accompany me to my horse."

Jason raised his eyebrows, but he pushed out his chair and stood. "Certainly." He cast a quick glance at Prudence and followed Jack.

When he returned a few minutes later, Prudence had cleaned the table, and the boys were settled doing lessons. Moses was reciting the alphabet very slowly, and Gideon was writing the letters on a slate. He had known none of his letters when he came to them. His ability to learn had stunned and delighted them all.

"Come, Pru. I must speak with thee."

Dread hit her in the stomach at his words, and she pulled her hands out of the hot soapy water. Drying her hands on her apron, she followed her husband onto the porch.

"What is it, Jason?"

"It is about something O'Hara discovered."

"About Gideon?"

He nodded. "His name is Tobias. They call him Toby."

"Toby." The name felt strange on her tongue. She shook her head. "We will continue to call him Gideon. Now, how did Jack discover this so-called information?"

"He was at the Wimber plantation across the river."

"The Wimber plantation?" Prudence could still vividly remember the night Rafe Wimber killed his brother Logan, who had fallen in love with a slave woman named Cecille and was running away with her. Jason had been forced to shoot Rafe to save Prudence.

"Yes," Jason said.

"So, what has Gideon to do with the Wimbers?"

Staring silently at her, Jason said more with his eyes and the thin line of his lips than he could have spoken aloud.

"Oh," she breathed. "I just assumed he had made a long journey. He was so starved and weary."

"Until he can speak to us, we will never know what he's gone through. He's been missing from the plantation since Wimber took him and his favorite dog off to war. Wimber returned three months after he left. His leg took a bullet, and he died of infection a couple of months later. Mrs. Wimber believes Toby died in the same battle."

That was a relief. The woman's assumption might be Toby's only hope to remain free until West Virginia and other border states loyal to the union were forced to comply with emancipation. For now, President Lincoln allowed for slaveholders in loyal states to keep their slaves.

"Apparently, our new friend Jack O'Hara is an opportunist. Once a week he sneaks across the river with goods he purchases. Flour, cornmeal, dried beans, dress goods, and other staples. He also sells vegetables during the season, and eggs to Miriam Wimber. Apparently, that woman has a secret market of sorts and sells—at a profit, of course—to her neighbors."

"Profiting from the misery of one's countrymen is indecent."

Jason shrugged. "I admit it is not how we would conduct ourselves, but we are still living in plenty compared to many of our Confederate neighbors, especially the women who have no men to care for them. Perhaps O'Hara's provisions are the only reason they are surviving."

"What should we do about this information? Will Miriam Wimber send someone to come looking for Gide—" She shook her head. "Toby, to her. Would he be safer in Canada?"

"I do not know."

"But are we certain Jack can be trusted? How did Miriam come to share this information with him?"

"Jack noticed a photograph of Mr. Wimber with a pack of dogs like Brown. Mrs. Wimber told him her husband took a dog and a boy with him when he left to go to war. It seemed all too clear she was talking about Toby and Brown."

"And what does he intend to do now? Turn Gideon over to her?" Clearly, their neighbor was not ashamed to profit from the ill fortunes of others. If Miriam offered a reward for the boy, would Jack betray them?

Right after lunch, the Abbotts went out for sightseeing while Karl and Shyla went to their room to look over video footage. Tess, LuAnn, and Janice helped clean up, then went upstairs to their sitting room with a slight detour for Janice, who stopped in the office to retrieve her copy of Prudence's journal.

"Okay, ladies, it's time," said Tess when Janice joined them. She and LuAnn had gotten their journal copies from their rooms and were getting comfortable on the couch. "Let's divide and conquer."

After determining who would look at what dates, silence reigned for a few minutes, broken only by the whistle of the teakettle Tess had put on the stove. She went to the kitchen, poured the hot water into three mugs, and delivered them to the coffee table along with a tray of assorted tea bags, sweeteners, and spoons.

"Here!" LuAnn jabbed a finger at the page in front of her. "Turn to May 12, 1863. Prudence mentions a Jack there."

Tess turned to the right page and read out loud from the entry.

For nigh unto two years now, this great war, this fight for freedom, has raged on, with no end in sight. And yet, in the midst of it all, we find life here in our little corner of the world has settled into a calm such as we have not experienced in many years, I fear we must fight off the temptation of complacency. I yearn to be of service to those still held in bondage despite the president's decree of emancipation. No parcels have come to us in over a year, and I suffer with the guilt of knowing we live in comfort and ease while others struggle still under the oppressive yoke of slavery. My dear husband is well aware of my double-minded heart. He tells me to be content rolling bandages and gathering goods for the soldiers and the wounded, that when the Good Lord has need of us for other tasks, He shall surely let us know.

I penned those words a month ago. So when our package arrived just days later, my heart was open and ready. Gideon is safe with us, and we are blessed with him. I must believe that Jack wishes him no harm and is diligently protecting Gideon's identity from those who would wish him enslaved once again. I pray daily for Jack, thankful for his loyalty and friendship. And today, as we celebrate our beloved son's fourth birthday, we hold on to a very tentative hope that God has brought us a second precious child to love and cherish as well.

When she finished reading it to the others, Tess looked up from her journal. "So, if this is Jack O'Hara, it seems, from what Prudence is saying, that he's not the kind of man to be a mobster."

"*If* this is the right Jack," agreed Janice. "I guess unless we find another Jack, this is the one Thelma and Irene are talking about."

Tess stretched back to ease the tension between her shoulder blades just as her phone rang.

She glanced at the screen. *Ed Baxter.*

"Hi, Ed. I'm sorry to have missed you yesterday. Apparently I waited too long."

"That's why I'm calling. I talked to LuAnn and Brad last night at the party. LuAnn told me you showed up in the afternoon to get your car. Sorry about that. We close at two on Fridays. Just to let you know I'll be here for a couple hours doing some paperwork if you want to come pick up your car."

"Sure, Ed. Thanks. I'll see if Janice or LuAnn can drive me over."

"Tess, there's one more thing." He paused as though formulating words.

"Yes?"

"It's just that Dane found something in one of our salvage cars. And I think you ought to know about it because the man who was driving it is staying at your place."

Curiosity washed over Tess like a wave. More than curiosity really. Ed sounded concerned. And that made her concerned as well.

She hung up and filled LuAnn and Janice in on Ed's call. Within fifteen minutes all three of them were in LuAnn's car and bound for Hilltop Auto Wrecking.

Ed unlocked the door at their knock. "I see you all came." He smiled, but Tess could tell there was tension at the corners of his mouth and in his jaw.

"First things first, Ed," she said. "Let me settle up the bill for my car, then we can talk."

"All right. I put in the new starter like we talked about. And Tess, your wiper blades were practically metal on glass, they were so worn down. When was the last time you had them replaced?"

"I'm not really sure."

"You need to stay up on those, or they'll do you no good in a rainstorm."

Tess gave him a salute. "Aye, aye, Captain."

He grinned. "I changed your oil too. You'd gone way over the recommended mileage. I'm not charging you for the blades or the oil since you didn't ask me to do those. We'll just call it a friend helping out a friend."

"Not on your life, Ed. I can't let you give me the blades and the oil. That costs you. Now, you tell me how much for the starter and labor and add in the other stuff you did."

"Now, Tess. I just said ..."

Setting her purse on the counter, Tess pulled out her checkbook. "I know you did it out of your good nature, and I appreciate it. But I should have gotten around to all that a lot sooner. You probably saved my engine."

Janice grinned. "Not to mention our necks next time we're out driving with Tess and the Lord sees fit to send us a sudden cloudburst."

Tess finally out-stubborned Ed. She handed him a check, and he handed her the keys to her car.

"Now," LuAnn said. "What did you find in Titus's car?"

"I suppose this is why all three of you came out here." He reached under the counter and pulled out a large manila envelope. "It's the strangest thing. Every time we think we've for sure cleaned out that old guy's car, something else turns up. These were stuffed down the back seat—like they'd been forgotten for a long time. I put them in an envelope to keep them together for Mr. Jones."

He opened the envelope and shook some newspaper clippings out on the counter in front of them. The clippings were yellowed and dog-eared, and some were badly torn. He picked one up by the corner and put it on top of the others.

"This is an article about a party given by Francine Kelly for a newly elected senator in New York some twenty years ago."

Tess nodded, recognizing Figgy dancing with a man she assumed was the senator.

"Now, look at this one." He set two articles side by side. The second one made Tess catch her breath. The same senator pictured dancing with Figgy at her home in New York had apparently been murdered. Ed read from the article. "'Senator Craig Railey was last seen alive in the home of Francine Kelly, wife of the late Nolan Kelly, who was believed to be tied to organized crime in the late sixties. Police say they have no suspects in the current case and do not believe the senator's presence at the party has any connection to his murder.'"

"Tess..." LuAnn tapped Tess's arm.

Ed shuffled through the stack of clippings. "Most of these are about the murder of the senator. There must be thirty or forty of them. Now why would Mr. Jones be carrying these around with him after all these years?"

"Tess! Janice!" LuAnn said more insistently.

"Wait a second, Lu," said Tess. She met Ed's gaze. "I'm not sure what you're getting at. Are you implying that Titus has some connection to the Kellys and the murdered senator?"

"I don't know what else to think," said Ed. "These were in his car."

LuAnn waved at them. "Will you two just look at this?" She pointed to the photo.

"What?" Tess said impatiently. "I see Figgy and the senator dancing."

"No," said LuAnn, pointing again. "Look in the background."

Tess and Janice peered past the dancing couple to a familiar man. He was two decades younger, but unmistakably recognizable.

Titus Jones.

CHAPTER TWELVE

Brad picked up the ladies of the Inn Crowd so they could ride together to church on Palm Sunday. The crowd was expected to be larger than the average Lord's Day, and Pastor Ben had requested the regular attendees carpool where it was convenient to do so to allow parking for visitors and latecomers.

Holding her hymnal, Tess lifted her voice and her heart as the choir sang in harmonious reflection of everything the season represented.

Living, He loved me
Dying, He saved me
Buried, He carried
My sins far away...

Pastor Ben preached a Palm Sunday sermon with such eloquence, Tess could almost see the palm leaves and hear the cries of *Hosanna! Blessed is He who comes in the name of the Lord!*

As they left the church, Tess felt like she could take in a full, deep breath for the first time in days. "Wasn't that a wonderful service?" she asked.

Janice and LuAnn carried palm branches that had been passed out to each member after the sermon. "I can't remember a better Palm Sunday service," Janice said. "Although I almost feel disloyal to Lawrence saying it."

Tess felt someone grab her arm as she followed her friends to the car. She turned to find Willa O'Hara standing next to her, pulling her back. "I need to talk to you," she said in a hushed tone.

Tess pulled her off the sidewalk, away from listening ears. "What's wrong, Willa?"

Willa's eyes were clouded with worry. "Would you say all of Winnie's staff for the party can be trusted?"

That was the last thing Tess expected to hear. "As far as I know, yes. The only person Winnie hired who doesn't work at the inn regularly is a college girl named Lana and one other student. Winnie knows their parents. They seemed okay. Why?"

"Something important went missing from Molly's house that night."

Tess's mind flashed back to all the jewels dripping from Molly the night of her birthday party. "I worried a little that that might happen with all the extra guests showing up. Did they get her diamonds?"

A crease appeared between Willa's eyes as she frowned, then her expression changed. "Oh, you mean her jewelry." She gave a little wave. "The real pieces are in a security deposit box at the bank. Gracious. The pieces she was wearing are replicas. If anyone stole them, they'd be in for a very disappointing reality check."

"Really? They fooled me."

"That's sort of the point." She smiled. "Anyway, it's not that jewelry we're missing."

"Then—"

Willa clamped her lips shut as Margaret Ashworth and Maybelline Rector walked by, deep in conversation. They offered cursory smiles when they noticed Willa and Tess.

"Beautiful solo this morning, Maybelline," Tess said.

Maybelline's eyebrows shot up, and her face brightened. "Thank you, Tess."

A sigh escaped Willa as the two ladies wandered out of earshot. "It's a family heirloom and also very valuable. Frankly, it's quite irreplaceable."

Tess glanced over Willa's shoulder and saw Janice and LuAnn waiting not so patiently with Brad by his car. "Why don't you just tell me what you're looking for, Willa? I can ask Winnie and her staff."

Willa shook her head. "No, you don't need to do that. I'm sure they didn't have anything to do with it. I don't know if you happened to see the locket that Gigi had on at the party. I tried to get her to take it off for one night, but she insisted on wearing it. Her sister Figgy left it to her when she passed, and Gigi hasn't taken it off since she got it a couple of weeks ago." She shook her head. "And now it's gone, and Gigi is frantic. And John is beside himself. I mean, if someone can come into a home where the police sergeant is, not to mention several other officers, and take a necklace right off his grandmother's neck, what does that say about his ability to protect his own family?"

"I think it says more about the thief than it does about Johnny, but I see what you're saying."

"I just don't know what to think about it going missing."

"Are you sure it didn't fall off her and onto the floor some-where? Maybe the chain broke?"

"We've combed the house, and we can't find it anywhere. The only explanation is that someone took it the night of the party. As I said, not only is it a valuable piece—it's worth a great deal of money because it's a very rare metal and very old—but the senti-mental value is immeasurable to Gigi. She's heartbroken."

"I'll let you know if I find out anything concrete, Willa. I need to go now. Janice and LuAnn are waiting for me with Brad."

She walked to the car, praying that what she was thinking wasn't true. Could Titus have stolen the locket? He had some kind of connection to the O'Haras and Kellys. For what pur-pose he would have done so, she couldn't begin to fathom. But there were too many connecting pieces for her to simply dismiss the idea.

<hr />

Tess decided to wait until after lunch to fill her friends in on the theft at Molly's. It weighed too heavily on her own mind as it was. There was no point burdening Janice and LuAnn until after lunch. Brad was eating with them, and he would most definitely notice if LuAnn didn't act normally.

They settled on their favorite Mexican restaurant and, after a short "church crowd" wait, they were settled at a table, eating homemade tortilla chips and salsa. Apparently they weren't the only members of Christ Fellowship to have a craving for Mexican food. Tess recognized several families, and, seated alone, Maybelline Rector looked ill at ease as she sipped water and perused the menu.

"For goodness' sake," Janice said. "One of us should go over there and invite her to join us."

"I could do it," Brad said.

"Thank you," LuAnn said. "But the invitation should come from one of us." She smiled at him. "Maybelline needs some socializing with other women, I think."

Brad grinned. "Should I leave?"

LuAnn chuckled. "No, you can stay, if you don't mind us adding another woman to the table."

Tess pushed out her chair. "I'll go." Maybelline glanced up and made eye contact as Tess walked to her table. Her eyes held a look of dread as though she already knew the question and was forming her answer.

"Hey, Maybelline." Tess touched the table. "Looks like we had the same idea for lunch."

"Looks like it." She gave a tight smile, but the wary look in her eyes remained. "I don't have any more information for you, if that's what you want to know, Tess."

Tess couldn't blame her for being suspicious of her motives. After all, how many times had she invited Maybelline just to eat and visit? She forced a smile, feeling the weight of her former lack of generosity toward Maybelline. "That's okay. We just wanted to invite you to join us."

"No," she said with no hesitation. "But thank you."

"You sure? I hate to see anyone eat alone."

Maybelline gave a short, humorless laugh. "Then you'd hate to see me about three meals every day."

Tess's face warmed. "If you change your mind, we haven't even ordered yet, so we'll be here a while. Again, your solo this morning was beautiful."

Maybelline's expression softened beneath the praise. "I wasn't too sure about that high C."

"You nailed it."

"Thanks to the Lord."

"You sure you won't join us?"

"I'm fine right here. But thank you." She nodded toward Tess's table. "Besides, it looks like you already have a full table."

Tess turned. Karl and Shyla had taken the last two seats at the table in the crowded restaurant. "We can squeeze you in if you change your mind. And we would love to talk to you sometime about what we found in Prudence's diary about Jack O'Hara and get your take on it—it's the May 12, 1863 entry."

She returned to her seat just as the server approached the table, ready to take their orders.

"What have you two been up to so far today?" Tess asked Karl after the short chaos of putting in their orders, surrendering their menus to the server, and waiting for her to head back to the kitchen.

"We drove past the O'Haras' place," Karl said. "Something is going on over there."

Tess thought back to the conversation with Willa, but she couldn't possibly say a word about the missing locket to a reporter hot on the trail of anything that would make a good story. "There always seems to be something going on over there."

"Tess, you were talking to Willa after church," Janice said. "Did she mention anything about Molly's place to you?"

"Well... Willa asked about the staff from Molly's party..."

Karl narrowed his gaze as he looked at her. "You know something."

Shyla placed her hand on his. "Don't tease her." She smiled. "Karl got his answer from one of the officers hanging around there this morning. They've gotten so used to seeing us sitting there, he walked right over to them and asked what was going on."

"Off the record." Karl shrugged. "It's not really news anyway. What did you hear, Tess?"

"Well..."

"How's your story about the mob coming along, Karl?" LuAnn asked.

Tess gave her a grateful smile for drawing Karl's attention away from her.

"It was stalling out, but things are looking up."

"Anything you can share with us?" Janice asked.

His eyes flashed with excitement. "I can't say much, obviously. But according to the officer I spoke to this morning, Molly O'Hara's nephew is going to be in town later today."

"Great-nephew," Shyla corrected.

"Right. Any guesses who he is?"

Janice shook her head. "I don't really know any of their extended family, and I grew up here in Marietta. Come to think of it, I can't remember hearing about any out-of-town visitors at the O'Haras' for years. Not since their heyday back in the sixties."

"I'll give you a hint," Karl said. "He's from New York."

LuAnn leaned forward. "Is he coming because of Molly's birthday?"

"That's one explanation for why he might be coming." A slight smile accompanied his cryptic answer, indicating he knew more than he was willing to say but he wanted them to know he had something up his sleeve. "He's the grandson of Nolan Kelly, the mob boss who was married to Molly O'Hara's sister, Figgy. His father was Lyle Kelly, who was just as notorious and ended up in prison during the seventies. He died in prison."

"So, the grandson must be around Johnny O'Hara's age. Is he married, have any kids?"

Karl shrugged. "All I know is his name is Anson. I've never found any record of a marriage or children for him. But I plan to try and get an interview with him, so maybe I'll ask about it." He grinned and crossed his fingers. "Here's hoping."

Tess glanced up as the server brought more chips and salsa. "Well, whatever the reason," she said, reaching for a chip, "I'm sure the O'Haras will be happy for a family visit."

Several minutes later, the server arrived carrying an enormous tray laden with sizzling plates of Mexican food. Conversation veered away from the O'Haras and the mob as they enjoyed their lunch.

The restaurant had already cleared out quite a bit, including Maybelline, by the time they finished, and LuAnn and Brad left together to spend the day antiquing.

Karl watched them leave and leaned in. "What's the story with those two?"

"They're just friends," Janice and Tess said together, then caught each other's eye and laughed. Until LuAnn was ready to admit there was a little more than friendship to her relationship with Brad, they certainly weren't going to spread romance rumors about their friend.

Karl rolled his eyes. "Sure they are."

"Hey, Karl," Tess said. "Since you're checking out tomorrow, do you two want to join us for dinner tonight? My daughter and her family are coming to grill burgers and hot dogs." It was still chilly in the evenings, but, according to Lizzie, Michael had been itching to grill.

Tess had no idea how on earth she would be hungry enough in five hours to eat supper after the enormous lunch she'd just had. But when her kids wanted to come over and bring her grands, she wasn't about to say no.

"That's nice of you, Tess," Karl said, sliding his arm along the back of Shyla's chair. "But I'm taking my beautiful wife out to a nice romantic dinner at the Buckley House."

Shyla smiled at him, then turned back to Tess and Janice. "I'm leaving tomorrow. I have to get back to work."

"What do you do?" Janice asked.

Tess focused on the fact that she had said "I'm leaving" not "We're leaving."

"I'm an ER nurse."

"She's being modest." Kyle practically vibrated with pride. "Shyla runs that place. They've been lost without her this week."

A modest blush darkened Shyla's cheeks. "He's a little prejudiced."

"Maybe, but that doesn't mean I'm not right."

"So, Karl," Tess said. "What time are the two of you planning to leave us tomorrow? I hope you leave time for breakfast. Winnie is making stuffed French toast."

Janice grinned. "And bacon."

"I actually wanted to talk to you, Tess," Karl said. "I can't leave yet. Not with Anson Kelly coming to town and the missing… Okay, I'll just tell you. My source at the police department told me a necklace was stolen from Molly O'Hara's house the night of her birthday party. I don't want to leave until I find out if there's a connection to Anson's visit."

"You're certainly welcome to stay," Tess said. "But I think you're reaching a little."

"Really?" Karl said in a tone that didn't sound at all pleased. "How so?"

Tess shrugged, trying to sound nonchalant. "I'm not sure how a locket missing from the mansion has anything at all to do with whether or not Molly's husband was tied to organized crime."

One side of Karl's mouth stretched upward. "Who said it was a locket?"

When Tess hesitated, Janice touched her arm and caught Karl's gaze. "Karl, do you plan to stay on in the honeymoon suite without Shyla? Or should we move you to another room?"

"I'd appreciate if I could move. The honeymoon suite would be a little lonely without my sweet honey."

Shyla laughed. "You're so cheesy."

Watching the two of them, it was easy to see that they loved each other very much. And it was easy to like Karl at the moment. Still, Tess knew they would all have to be a lot more careful around him not to say anything about Titus or the missing locket or the newspaper articles. Karl might be a better man than Tess had ever imagined, but he was still a reporter, and if Shyla was his first love, getting elbow deep into a story was a close second.

CHAPTER THIRTEEN

May 18, 1863

Prudence tried to hide her anxiety over discovering that the plantation where Gideon had come from was merely ten miles on the other side of the river, but the tension in the house was nearly palpable. For a week, she had jumped at nearly every noise—in particular when Brown let out his keening hound howl.

They hadn't seen Jack O'Hara during the past week either, and that was also disconcerting. They had spoken of the situation in hushed tones away from the boys so they were not overheard.

Gideon seemed to sense there was more to O'Hara's absence than his usual comings and goings, and he genuinely seemed to miss the man. He cast his gaze toward the door every morning, obviously hoping to see and hear their boisterous neighbor inviting himself to breakfast. Prudence went to bed each night that week with a prayer on her lips for wisdom.

On the eighth day after learning the truth about Gideon, she stumbled out of bed before dawn to start breakfast.

While the biscuits baked, she poured her coffee and quietly stepped onto the porch. She sat in the rocking chair and watched while the sky across the tree line became lighter, then suddenly burst with color.

"What a beautiful world Thee has provided—"

"Who are you talkin' to?"

Startled, Prudence gasped and jumped to her feet, spilling her coffee. Jack O'Hara stood at the end of the porch, and only his head and shoulders were visible through the rails.

"Jack!" She picked up her empty cup and noticed that coffee had splashed onto the hem of her only clean everyday dress. She would have to do the wash a day early, and that did not please her one bit.

"Did I scare you, Mrs. Willard?"

"I should say so."

"Sorry." He had walked around to the steps as they spoke. He trudged up them, his battered hat clutched between his meaty hands. "I just don't recall ever hearing a woman pray out loud that way. My sister says prayers are in her heart and just between her and the Almighty." He grinned. "I figure most of those are asking Him to do something about me."

She certainly wouldn't doubt the truth of that. "God looks at the heart and hears what we think, whether we ever speak a prayer or not. And I might have kept my prayer private as well, had I known I had an audience other than God."

"Yes, ma'am. I should've spoke up."

"Jack. Why was thee lurking about?" And why hadn't Brown barked to announce him? Then she noticed the dog was gnawing on a bone of some sort.

He shrugged. "Shot myself a deer last week. Thought I'd bring the mutt a bone to keep him quiet."

"I am sure he appreciates it. But I must ask thee again. Why was thee lurking? Thee is welcome here any time."

"That's kind of you. But I think I'm being watched. I didn't want to get you folks into any trouble with...anyone."

Prudence smiled. "Would thee like some coffee? We could have some out here on the porch until the family awakens."

"If it's not too much trouble."

Prudence refilled her cup and poured his, sweetening it with nearly the last of her sugar, which, along with coffee, was getting more difficult to come by. She pulled the biscuits from the oven to cool and started water boiling for oats. The boys didn't like oats as much as other breakfasts. But with a little brown sugar and cream, they were willing to eat it, and it was filling.

Jack had taken the second rocking chair, but as Prudence returned, he stood as gracefully as his girth would allow and took his cup. "Thank you, kindly."

"Thee is most welcome. Please sit."

His eyes held a weariness, and dark half-moon shadows appeared below them.

"Thee was saying about being watched...?" A man in his business likely would be anxious, considering it was illegal to move food from the Union into Confederate hands, and while part of Virginia had remained loyal to the Union, the Wimbers certainly weren't.

But these were things she couldn't bring herself to ask. Perhaps she didn't want to know the truthful answer.

"I'm not a good man like your husband."

"Jack, no one is good, except the Lord. We each do our best every day and still lie down at night knowing we have failed many times."

He frowned and tilted his head at her. "You're just trying to make me feel better."

"Is thee accusing me of falsehood?"

"No, ma'am. But I've been watching you and your man ever since that boy showed up. My pa used to call people like you folks 'go maith.'" He smiled at her confused look at the words, which sounded like *guh mah* to her. "In the Irish, it means 'good folks.'"

"That is very kind of thee to say." She reached out with a boldness she typically did not display and touched his arm. "But remember, Jack, only God is good. That is why we are not consumed by the fires of this life and blown away by its storms."

He narrowed his gaze and seemed to consider her words. "Ma'am, I don't mean to upset you, but I just have to think maybe this God of yours is better to some than others."

Compassion twisted in Prudence's heart for the man who showed more goodness than he obviously knew. But she had to wonder at his words. Did he harbor some secret pain that only God could heal?

"He loves us all the same. Even thee, Jack."

"I'd best be going. Sun's almost all the way up." With a grunt he hauled himself from the chair.

Surprised, she stood as well. "Thee won't be joining us for breakfast?"

"No, ma'am. Like I said, I'm being watched, and it won't do you or the boy any good if they see you welcoming me into your home."

And he thought he wasn't a good man? As she watched him walk down the steps, Prudence wanted to tell him that only someone endowed with compassion put others before himself. But he paused when he reached the bottom and turned. "I know you believe God is good, Mrs. Willard. And an old sinner like me can't fault someone like you for believin' that." He pointed to the door. "But I reckon that boy sleeping in there by the fireplace might think a little different about that than you do."

The smell of the first cookout of the year tempted Tess's senses despite the large lunch she'd had just hours ago. She, LuAnn, Janice, and Lizzie sat lazily on the patio with Titus, who had gratefully accepted the invitation to eat dinner with them. Besides Karl, Titus was the only guest at the inn for the night, so it seemed like the right thing to do to invite him to join them.

Michael, Tess's son-in-law, flipped burgers on the grill. The triplets played in the yard with Huck, who barked and ran after balls and sticks and the nearly four-year-olds. But Henry was clearly Huck's favorite. His energy was boundless and matched Huck's.

Titus chuckled watching Huck and the triplets playing. "I'm trying to decide which of those two will outlast the other."

Lizzie laughed. "It looks like Liam and Harper are already getting tired of the game, and Huck is starting to pant. I'm guessing Henry is going to be the winner."

"Lizzie," Michael called. "Can you get me a platter? These are about done."

Standing, Lizzie stretched her back and headed for the door. "Will you keep an eye on the kids, Mom?"

"Of course."

"Having grandchildren must be the greatest gift," Titus said, his tone pensive.

Watching the triplets running in the yard, playing with Huck, Tess nodded. "It is. There's something even more special about it than having your own kids."

"I concur," Janice piped in.

"I wouldn't know," LuAnn said. "But I get to be the fun great-aunt to all of their grandkids."

Titus chuckled. "So it's true what they say about grandkids. Love them, spoil them, then send them home?"

"Something like that."

Lizzie returned, carrying the platter. In a minute, it was filled with sizzling burgers. "Where are we eating tonight?" Michael asked Tess.

Tess turned to Lizzie. "Where did you put the potato salad and green beans you brought?"

"In the refrigerator down here."

Tess shrugged. "We might as well eat in the downstairs kitchen then."

She started to get up, but Lizzie put a hand on her shoulder. "All of you just relax for a little bit while we set the table. If you don't mind watching the triplets for a little while longer."

"You know I don't mind."

When she had gone, Titus leaned forward, resting his elbows on his knees. "Ladies, since all three of you are here," he said slowly, "there's something I think I should tell you—"

The sound of barking and growling followed by high-pitched yelps invaded the calm, peaceful evening. Henry screamed. It all happened so fast, they were on their feet and across the yard in a split second.

Somehow, Titus reached the commotion before the women. A dog Tess had never seen had found its way into the yard and had attacked poor little Huck. A few jabs of Titus's cane scared him off, leaving Huck lying on the ground. Tess knelt on the grass, and Henry fell into her arms, crying.

"Mom!" Lizzie and Michael must have heard the head-spinning sudden noise and arrived in the yard seconds after the rest of them. The parents scooped up the other two crying children. "What happened?"

"I don't know," Tess said. "It happened so fast."

"Huck is hurt." LuAnn's voice trembled as she stared down at the dog lying on the ground and whining softly.

Titus dropped his cane, took off his jacket, and wrapped up Huck while speaking softly to him. Leaving the cane where it had fallen, he carried him into the house with a pronounced limp. Tess led the way. "Where can we take him?"

"Upstairs," Janice said. "You can put him on the kitchen table."

"I'll take the elevator," he said, grimly, cradling Huck.

Lizzie and Michael led the children into the library to shield them from the awful situation.

The women didn't speak as they hurried up the steps.

"I've seen that stray on our walks," LuAnn said, her voice still shaking as she opened the suite's main door. "He never seemed threatening before." They hung back, allowing Titus to precede them inside. LuAnn had grabbed Titus's cane from where he'd dropped it on the ground. She laid it at the other end of the kitchen table.

Janice went straight to her linen closet and grabbed towels to spread on the table.

"Should I call the emergency line for the vet?" Tess asked.

"Call them." Titus carefully laid the limp dog on the towels. "I don't have time to explain right now, but I can take care of him, if you ladies will trust me. I'll try to make sure he's stable enough for us to get him to the pet hospital."

With Huck in such bad shape, now wasn't the time to question Titus. How long had he known this? Did he have all his memory back, or just what he did for a profession? "Tess, while she makes the call, will you please bring me a tub or pan or something with warm water so I can wash his wounds and check how bad they are?" He turned to Janice. "Do you have bandages and a first aid kit?"

While Tess and Janice retrieved the supplies Titus had asked for, LuAnn made the call. "I got their voice mail. But I left a message. They should call back soon."

Titus had rolled up his sleeves, and he began to wash Huck's wounds. He pulled his key from his pocket and turned to Tess. "Will you please go to my room? There's a black bag on the shelf in the closet. Bring it to me, please."

Without hesitation, Tess grabbed the key. She flew down the steps and unlocked his third-floor room. She went straight to the closet and reached for the bag. As her hand closed around soft leather, her eye caught another item on the shelf. The newspaper clippings Ed had shown them. And the one on top...

There was no time to think about that now. There was only Huck and saving the little fellow's life. She hurried out of Titus's room and headed back upstairs, breathing heavily once she reached their door.

In moments, the black bag was open on the table, along with the first aid kit. They stood back to give Titus the best light, but the poor dog's quiet whimpers elicited tears from Janice and LuAnn. Tess had to fight back emotion.

"The good news, ladies, is that none of these wounds are jagged or deep enough for stitches, which is a relief, as there doesn't seem to be an analgesic in my bag. Two of them should heal fine with a disinfecting agent and a bandage. These three though..." He showed them a cut on Huck's leg, one on his side, and one on his ear. "A few years ago, I'd have stitched these. The one on his side, at least. But these days I prefer to use a skin glue. It'll keep the wound closed so it can heal without much risk of infection, and the glue will absorb into his skin."

"That's a relief," Tess said.

As they watched him work, the three women exchanged silent glances. Tess could imagine they were all thinking the same thing. Clearly, Titus didn't even realize he was revealing a recovered memory. Or...did he?

Now wasn't the time to question his past. They needed to let him do his work.

Seemingly oblivious to anything but Huck, Titus worked gently, speaking softly to the little dog. "It's okay, boy. You'll be okay."

In less than an hour, Titus had finished dressing Huck's wounds. "There we go. He's all fixed up. Probably ought to try to get him to take it easy for a couple of days at least. He'll be sore. And I'd get him some water to replace the fluids he's lost."

Huck stood up on shaky legs as though he knew Titus was finished. LuAnn carefully scooped him into her arms. "Oh, my poor boy. Should we take him to the hospital when they call back?"

Titus shrugged. "It might not hurt to make an appointment with your regular vet tomorrow, but I'd say the emergency is over."

Tess started cleaning up the mess while Titus rolled his shirt sleeves back down. He picked up his blood-spotted jacket. "I don't suppose you can recommend a good dry cleaner?"

Tess smiled and took the jacket from him. "We'll get it cleaned for you. It's the least we can do after you patched up our dog." She observed the fatigue lining his face. "Can I get you some tea or something, Titus?"

He shook his head. "I think I'll head back to my room and stretch out my leg."

Tess reached out and laid a hand on his arm. "We're glad you were here and knew exactly what to do. We thank you."

"Titus..." Janice began. "How did you—"

The sound of LuAnn's ringtone silenced her. Tess opened the door for Titus and watched as he limped to the elevator. When she shut the door, she turned to LuAnn, who had just hung up and was still cradling Huck. "Was that the pet hospital?"

LuAnn nodded. "I told them what happened but explained we have everything under control. We'll call the vet in the morning. They'll need to check him for rabies. I didn't even think about that. But he should be up to date on all his shots."

"I better go down and let my grandchildren know Huck's going to be fine."

Tess found them in the library, the children lying across Lizzie's and Michael's laps, sound asleep. Lizzie glanced up as Tess walked into the room. "How's Huck?"

She filled them in, and Lizzie's face softened with relief. "Poor Henry. He feels responsible."

"Why?" Tess's heart swelled with love as she looked at her grandchildren.

"He says Huck was protecting him."

Alarm seized her. "Did the other dog go after the kids?"

"I don't know. I don't think Henry knows. He just saw that dog, and Huck went ballistic. He must have thought the kids were in danger."

"We'll call animal control tomorrow. I hate to. But I don't see what else we can do." She looked at the kids again. "Did they eat?"

Lizzie shook her head. "Too upset. I wrapped up some burgers to take home. I made a plate for Mr. Jones too. And there's food for you to take upstairs for you three. Everything is cleaned up. We've just been waiting to hear about Huck. We'll take the kids home now."

Tess waited downstairs while Michael and Lizzie got the triplets loaded into their car. When they left, the place felt suddenly empty. She grabbed a bag and packed up the food Lizzie had set aside for them. Then she went to the third floor and knocked on Titus's door. When he didn't come to the door, she knocked again, but there was still no answer.

Taking his plate with her, she headed back upstairs to the apartment. LuAnn and Janice sat in the living room. "Titus didn't come to the door," Tess said. "I was going to drop off this plate Lizzie made for him."

"Maybe he fell asleep." LuAnn glanced at Huck on the couch where she'd made him a bed. When Tess followed her gaze, LuAnn smiled. "He didn't seem comfortable with me holding him. I thought he'd rest better this way."

"I have food here. Are you hungry?" Tess walked to the kitchen and set the food on the counter. She set the oven to warm up the hamburgers and pulled three plates from the cabinet.

"Don't worry," Janice said. "I cleaned and disinfected the table. We can eat there."

A few minutes later, as they sat at the table, Janice and LuAnn exchanged a glance.

"Okay, Tess," LuAnn said. "Time to spill it. I can tell you have something on your mind."

"I think we all do. It's been a rough day."

"I'm not just talking about what happened to Huck," LuAnn said. "I'm talking about what Karl said. What's this about a necklace being taken?"

Tess sighed and set her fork down. "Okay. Willa told me about the necklace after church today."

LuAnn stopped her. "Should I get my notebook?"

"It might not hurt."

She was back in a flash.

"You saw me talking to Willa after church."

LuAnn sat, pen poised over notebook. "Yes. She looked a little upset."

Janice sipped her tea. "Which is a pity after such a beautiful service."

Tess took a deep breath and spoke on the exhale. "They think the theft happened at the party the other night."

"I'm not surprised," Janice said. "The way Molly was flashing those jewels."

LuAnn looked up. "Yes, but at ninety-five, when does she have the chance to wear them?"

"That's true."

Tess sipped her tea, savoring the spicy aroma steaming from the mug. "Those were replicas anyway. The real ones are in a bank somewhere."

"Then what's the point?" Janice asked.

"Who knows?" Tess shrugged and looked from one to the other.

"You said it was a locket that was taken," LuAnn nudged.

"This isn't the best news for Titus, considering…" Tess paused to gather her thoughts. "It was a very valuable antique locket. It was missing at the end of the party."

LuAnn frowned at her. "What's that got to do with Titus?"

Tess took a deep breath. "Well…when I went up to get Titus's bag for him, the newspaper clippings were there, right beside it. The one on top was an article about a locket that Figgy Kelly had gotten from her husband for their fortieth anniversary, right before he died. From what Willa told me, it's a very rare and valuable piece."

Janice covered her mouth with her hand, her eyes widening. LuAnn's expression changed instantly from curiosity to dread.

"Oh, no," LuAnn said. "What are the odds?"

Tess nodded. "Exactly."

Janice's expression showed disbelief. "Titus was with you all evening, Tess. How could he have stolen the locket?"

"He wasn't with me every second."

A frown creased Janice's brow. "Like when?"

"Think about it."

"Oh. Nature's call. Okay, but that doesn't mean he's the one who took the locket."

LuAnn spoke while she wrote. "But it does look a little suspect, Janice. I know you want to believe in Titus. But between the newspaper articles, the senator's murder, and now the missing locket..." She shrugged. "I don't know what to think anymore."

"Did you see the money when you got the bag?" Janice asked, her tone eager.

"I didn't exactly have time to look around with Huck injured."

"Oh, true."

LuAnn wrote in the notebook, then looked up. "Should we confront him?" she asked in a low tone.

Janice fixed her gaze on LuAnn. "Of course we shouldn't. We can't accuse him of stealing and who knows what else without more proof. It could all end up being a coincidence, and we would have upset him for nothing."

Tess nodded in agreement. "Janice is right. Plus, if we do confront him, I imagine he'd pack up and leave before we have any real answers."

Janice pursed her lips in thought just before she spoke. "Maybe that's what Titus wanted to talk to us about anyway."

"Titus wanted to talk to us?" LuAnn said. "Oh, you mean right before Huck was hurt."

The memory of him sitting forward and about to speak flashed across Tess's mind. "There's so much we don't know about him, he could have been about to tell us anything. He did seem serious. For that matter, he might have been wanting to tell us he's moving on after all."

"Or that he has a bag of money," Janice offered.

"Or that he stole a locket." LuAnn's eyes glinted with humor.

"Or that he has a much younger lady friend," Tess said, taking up the same humorous tone.

"Oh, I forgot about her," Janice said. "From the coffee shop." Her expression became thoughtful. "Maybe he wanted to tell us he's gotten his memory back. We know he must be a veterinarian or something very close to it. And he remembered that he used to use stitches but now he uses skin glue."

Tess sobered at the mention of how he was obviously beginning to remember some things.

"Tess," LuAnn said, "maybe we should give him a chance to open up to us again. But if he doesn't, it might not hurt to call Agent Butler again and give him more details this time. With FBI resources he would probably have better luck figuring out where Titus came from."

Tess hesitated. On the one hand, she had grown fond of Titus over the past week and didn't want to do anything to cause trouble for him—especially now that he'd saved Huck. On the other hand, too many things weren't adding up, and he seemed to be the common factor in each problem. If he had brought danger to the inn and the people she loved, Tess had to believe it was worth a little meddling to get to the bottom of the mystery of Titus Jones.

CHAPTER FOURTEEN

May 19, 1863

"Mama?"

At the sound of Moses's voice, Prudence came instantly awake. She sat up. "What is it, dear?" she whispered.

"Gideon's gone."

"What do you mean?"

"He's not there."

She swung her legs around the side of the bed to stand and pressed her finger to her lips with a cautious look at Jason still sleeping on his side of the bed.

She reached the living room and glanced at the pallet in front of the fire. Gideon's rumpled bedding remained, but he was gone. "Did thee check the outhouse?"

Moses nodded. "That's where I went first."

Placing her hand on her son's head, she said, "Did thee see Brown?"

"He's gone too."

With her heart beating wildly in her chest, Prudence stepped onto the porch where the sky was beginning to lighten as dawn approached. There was no sign of the boy or the dog. Her stomach dropped, and panic began to set in. "Dear Father," she prayed aloud as she rushed down the steps, "have mercy on the child Thee sent."

A clear set of fresh wagon tracks stretched out in front of the house. She turned to Moses. "Go and rouse thy papa."

Moses rushed back inside as Prudence saw the tracks heading down the road. Had Jack O'Hara betrayed them? This was a man who had sat at their table, sat on this very porch with her sharing deeper-than-surface thoughts, a man she truly believed was getting close to knowing God, a man who had gained their trust and, more importantly, had gained Gideon's trust. Had he truly taken the boy back into a life at the Wimber plantation, and all for worldly gain?

Oh, Lord. Please, may it not be so.

Tess was relieved to walk into the café the next morning and find Titus sitting in his usual spot drinking his coffee. He smiled when he saw her and set his coffee cup on the table. "Good morning," he said. "How's Huck today?"

"He seems better. At least he got up and walked to his food bowl."

Titus's eyes lit up. "That's a good sign."

"The vet heard about our message last night and called LuAnn this morning. She told LuAnn to bring Huck in so she can check him out before the clinic opens. Apparently her day is packed after nine."

Robin walked through the kitchen door carrying a tray with Titus's breakfast. She smiled when she saw Tess. "Thank goodness. Someone I can wait on. It's so slow this morning. I don't have any rooms to clean or, as you can see, many guests to wait on. Please, let me get your coffee and breakfast."

Tess grinned back. "It's the least I can do."

"Will you join me?" Titus asked.

She sat in the chair he indicated. "How did you sleep last night?" she asked him. "I brought you some supper, but you must have already gone to bed."

He shook his head and met her gaze. "I went out to meet someone."

"Oh. I see." Tess's mind conjured up the image of the woman he'd been standing with at the door of Jeremiah's the other night. He had a perfect right to go wherever he chose.

But after he'd said his leg was hurting and he needed to stretch it, she'd just assumed he wouldn't be going out.

"I've been meaning to thank you for the plant you left in my room on Friday." He smiled. "Forget-me-nots seem appropriate, considering."

Tess frowned. "Plant? I don't remember anyone mentioning that to me. But Janice might've done it. She's pretty thoughtful that way."

"Then I suppose she's the one I should thank."

Robin brought Tess's coffee and breakfast and set it down in front of her. "Winnie said there's plenty where this came from if either of you want more."

"Robin, hang on a sec."

"Something wrong?"

Shaking her head, Tess pointed to Titus. "Do you remember putting forget-me-nots in Titus's room Friday?"

Her face brightened as she nodded. "They were delivered. No card. Just the delivery tag. I was going to clean your room, so I just took them on up." A tiny frown creased her brow. "I–I hope that was okay? I just assumed—"

"It's fine, of course," Titus said, though his face had clouded at the news. "Well, I see I still have a mystery."

Robin glanced at Tess. "I better get back to the kitchen. We're fixing a pot of vegetable beef soup, and I have the task of chopping all the vegetables."

Tess waited until she was out of earshot before turning back to Titus. "Titus, last night you took great care of Huck.

Are you a veterinarian? I don't mean to pry, but it does seem like your memory is starting to return."

He nodded. "It started coming back, just flashes here and there, a few days ago. Then, when Huck got hurt, I remembered how to take care of his wounds." With a heavy sigh, he leaned back in his seat. "But that's not all. Molly O'Hara isn't the only person I've met in the last week who thinks she knows me." His words came out heavily, as though it was an effort just to speak. "Thursday night, while you three ladies were at your choir practice, I walked to the coffeehouse just down from the inn. I like to go in there. It's peaceful. I was reading my Bible when a woman approached my table. She called me Mickey."

Tess sucked in a breath. "Oh my goodness."

"At first I told her she must have me confused with someone else. Even though she seemed sincere and insisted that I had disappeared four months ago."

"Who is she, Titus?"

He held up his hands and put them back on the table. "She said I'm a veterinarian and that she used to work with me in Morristown, New Jersey."

"And she came all this way to find you?" That was pretty dedicated for a coworker.

He shrugged. "I don't understand it all myself. And I didn't give her much of a chance to explain further."

"It seems like she might have given you the answers you've been looking for."

He shook his head. "What she was saying didn't make sense to me. Like you just said, why would a coworker travel over four hundred miles to find me? But she was insistent that I'm a veterinarian from New Jersey, and my name is Mickey Truitt. I wasn't sure whether to believe her or not, and I panicked. When she wouldn't leave me alone, I finally took her cell phone number but told her I needed a couple of days to think things over and contact my psychiatrist."

That explained the belligerent body language they'd noticed from the car. "You didn't ask her any questions?"

"I know it sounds crazy, considering I've felt like a blank slate for four and a half months. But yesterday, when I suddenly knew what to do with Huck, I decided to give her a call and try to find out more about my past. She agreed to meet me. She's the one I was talking about when I said I went to meet someone."

"And did you—"

She was going to ask if he had recovered more memories or at least more information about himself. But before she could get the question out, she heard the unmistakable sound of a fire truck siren. Seconds later, Janice poked her head into the café. "Is there a fire? Justin O'Hara just pulled up with a crew."

"There's no fire that I know of."

"I better go see what he's doing. There's a big fire truck and the chief's pickup parked outside."

"I'll come with you," Tess said. She turned to Titus. "Excuse me, Titus, I need to see about this. Can we finish this talk later?"

"Yes, of course. I have exciting news for you." He smiled.

Tess headed toward the front door, making a mental note to get back to the conversation with Titus as soon as she possibly could.

Justin O'Hara's wide grin greeted Tess and Janice as they stepped onto the porch. Three burly men hopped down from the fire truck.

"Where do you want all this candy?" Justin asked.

The ladies stepped off the porch and looked in the bed of the pickup where they saw four big barrels, chock-full of candy.

"Goodness gracious goat," Janice breathed out. "How did you collect that much candy in a month?"

"People like to donate to causes firefighters take up. We put it in the newspaper a couple of weeks ago and have had a steady stream of donations ever since." Justin grinned. "The chief said he's tired of tripping over chocolate, so here we are."

Tess looked at Janice. "Where are we going to put it all?"

Janice paused, and lines of concentration creased her brow. "We can put two in the office. In the corners with the eggs. And I suppose we can take the other two upstairs."

The door opened, and Karl stepped outside. Trotting down the steps, he joined them next to the pickup. He looked as though he'd just rolled out of bed as he swiped at his hair. He glanced at Tess. "That's Justin O'Hara?"

"Good morning, Karl," she said, realizing she was using a tone she might have used with one of her students for not greeting her properly before launching into a question.

"Good morning. I heard the commotion."

"Yes, that's Justin. Didn't you meet him at Molly's?"

He shook his head. "I kept missing him." He shrugged. "I think he was avoiding me."

"He was preoccupied making sure Molly's house stayed up to fire code standards, with so many people packed in there." Tess pointed to the back of the pickup. "The firefighters have been collecting candy for the Easter egg hunt this weekend."

Karl shoved his hands into his pockets. "That's nice." He sounded distracted as he watched Justin. Clearly, he was dying to gather O'Hara information from the youngest member of the family.

"Justin, can your men carry those barrels in for us?" Janice called out.

"Yes, ma'am. That's the plan. Just tell us where you want them."

Each firefighter muscled a barrel from the back of the pickup. They followed Janice and Tess into the inn. "It's on the fourth floor. Do you want to take the stairs or the elevator?"

Justin grinned. "We're firefighters," he said with his swaggering flair. "Walking up four flights of stairs is like a walk in the park for us."

"Have it your way," Janice said. "But it might not be so easy carrying all that candy."

He winked. "We've got it covered, Miss Janice."

"If you say so. Two of you follow me upstairs. Two follow Tess."

"You can bring those into the office," Tess said, focusing her gaze on the two older firefighters, who, in unspoken agreement, had chosen not to take the "walk in the park" to the fourth floor.

She turned to see Karl following Justin up the stairs. Likely, he wanted to grill the poor boy about the criminal acts of the Family O'Hara. The firefighters and Janice were back within a few minutes. Janice walked by Tess with a little wave. "I'm going to see if anyone needs my help in the kitchen," she said.

Justin walked to the check-in desk. "My mom said you wanted me to ask the chief about parking a fire truck here during the Easter EGGstravaganza."

"That's right. We did mention it to her." With everything happening over the past few days, Tess had forgotten all about it.

"I have good news. The chief said we can bring the truck on Saturday and let the kids take turns sitting inside. I think they might like that."

"That's a terrific idea, letting them get inside the truck. Are you going to be the one to give them the honor, or will it be someone else?"

He grinned again. "I'll be doing it. And the honor is all mine."

From the corner of her eye, Tess saw Karl approaching. He must've gone to his room because his hair was wet like he'd at least smoothed it down. He held out his hand to Justin. "Hi. I'm Karl," he said.

Justin shook Karl's hand, but Tess could see that he had thrown up his guard.

"I recognize you."

Karl must have noted his wariness too, although Tess had to think the reporter was used to people being guarded whenever he was around. Still, Karl wasn't the type to be thrown off by a little bit of an icy reception. "How is your grandmother?"

"My grandmother lives in Chicago." Justin winked at Tess. "And she had pneumonia, but she seems to be bouncing back."

"Oh, right. I meant Molly."

"Gigi? She's the sweetest."

"Did your uncle make it into town okay?" Now he was getting to the point. Tess could almost feel Karl's anticipation mixed with frustration that Justin wasn't cooperating.

"If you mean Anson, he's more like a second cousin or third cousin something or other removed. I've never been able to keep those straight. How about you, Miss Tess? Are you a historian?"

"Not really," she mumbled, preferring to stay out of the fray. "That's LuAnn."

They heard a loud honk from the fire truck. "Okay," Justin said, "that's my ride. Time to go back to the firehouse. We're washing all the trucks today."

Karl turned and matched Justin's stride. "I'll walk you out. So, you never answered about your...Anson Kelly..."

With a shake of her head, Tess opened the online reservations page for the inn. Including Karl and Titus, the rooms at the inn would be full tonight. Unusual for a Monday. She heard voices coming from the direction of the café and looked away from the computer as Titus and Janice walked toward the counter.

"I was just telling Titus about all the candy those men brought."

"Seems you ladies are going to be busy this week." Titus smiled. "I'd be happy to help out where I can."

"We might take you up on that," Janice said with a laugh. "Tess ordered six thousand plastic eggs."

"In my defense, we are likely to have five hundred or more kids throughout the day. I'd rather have too many than see a child walk away without a basketful of treats."

"Hear, hear," Titus said.

"And there's something for adults too." Janice's eyes shone as she spoke about the upcoming EGGstravaganza. "We're sponsoring an Easter bonnet contest."

"Janice's brainchild," Tess said. "The events coordinator at Bend-of-the-River Retirement Center used last week's craft day, and is using this week's too, to help the women create their bonnets. It should be fun."

Janice beamed. "Besides the ladies from the retirement center, we have nearly every women's group in town signed up—even some younger women, like from the Mothers of Preschoolers group. And also the ladies of the Catholic Women's club, who've been coming to the inn during Lent because Winnie makes a fish-based soup every Friday during the season. There'll be a lot of activities for the children, like bouncy houses and face painting."

All in all, the day had the potential to be either a huge success or a crushing failure, as God willed. But they were doing everything they could to provide a service to the children of Marietta and the surrounding area.

Janice leaned toward Titus. "We're even putting some valuable prizes in a few of the plastic eggs. First prize is a night at the inn with a guest. Second and third prizes are lunch at the inn." She shrugged. "I wanted to give away a piece of antique silver for the second prize, but the others thought it might be too extravagant for the occasion."

Titus smiled. "I can say from experience that the winners are going to be very happy with their prizes. Whether they win a night as a guest or a complimentary lunch."

Tess wished she could find a smooth way to return to the conversation she had been having with Titus when the firefighters showed up. But unfortunately, for now at least, he seemed more interested in small talk. Maybe he regretted opening up about the woman in Jeremiah's Coffee House in the first place. Or he just needed to keep his thoughts to himself.

Either way, there was no doubt that Titus Jones was about to walk out of the darkest recesses of missing memory into the light of the truth about himself. The question was, what would that shining light of truth reveal about the kind of man Titus really was?

CHAPTER FIFTEEN

May 19, 1863

The day dawned beautifully, but for Prudence, the skies might as well have been gray and dreary as they dressed quickly, loaded Moses into the wagon, and followed the trail left by the fresh wagon tracks. It would have been faster if Jason had gone himself, but she couldn't just sit by and do nothing.

As they followed the tracks toward the river, Prudence couldn't help but feel a twinge of relief. When they reached the bank of the river, the tracks turned rather than stopping to take the skiff to the Virginia side of the Ohio. She watched the water as they continued to follow the tracks. She had taken countless trips across the river in the dead of night, in rain, wind, snow. She pictured the faces of weary men and women and the wide eyes of terrified children. There had been so many snatched from the hands of bondage. Had they lost the last child God had sent them?

The distinct sound of a bark that could only have come from a bloodhound reached them. Jason turned to her and, with the unspoken agreement between them, he turned the wagon toward the sound.

Father, she prayed, *please guide us.*

She wanted Gideon. She had grown to love him as her own and would gladly raise him in their home, countering all the questions from well-meaning neighbors over the wisdom of becoming a mother to a dark-skinned child. She and Jason would likely be forced to reveal the truth of their own origin. That they were not fully white, though they had always lived that way. A few trusted friends knew the truth, of course. But Prudence had escaped from slavery, had been adopted herself, and God had used her past bondage to give her the path her life was to take. Perhaps God had indeed rewarded her with a second child at the end of the journey.

Nevertheless, Thy will be done.

Prudence's heart nearly stopped as they reached the sound of Brown's warning barks. Outside of the Riverfront House, Gideon held on to the dog where they sat in the back of a wagon. They were surrounded by no less than a dozen Union soldiers on horseback.

The rest of Monday passed so quickly, Tess barely had time to catch her breath. The lunch crowd filled up the café, and it stayed a whirlwind of activity until they ran out of soup thirty minutes before they normally finished lunch. Guests checked in at a staggered pace, keeping them hopping.

It was after four before she had her afternoon cup of coffee and retreated to the office to do paperwork. But her mind was too filled with Titus, the woman in the coffeehouse, Huck, and a hundred other things, and distraction plagued her. It was a welcome relief when Taylor tapped on her door just after five. Glancing up, she smiled. With Taylor on spring break from classes, they had increased his hours this week. He and Robin were tasked with filling plastic eggs whenever they had a free moment.

"What's up, Taylor?"

"Sorry to interrupt, but there's a woman here to see you, Janice, and LuAnn."

"Oh? I wasn't expecting anyone." The others weren't either. LuAnn was spending the rest of the day tending Huck and filling eggs with Janice.

Maybelline peeked around Taylor, tension tightening her face. "I made time for you and your friends, so you can certainly take a few minutes for me."

"Of course. Come in, Maybelline."

Maybelline glanced around, and Tess realized the woman hadn't been to the inn since they'd bought it and done the remodel. Tess held her breath, bracing herself for a snarky comment from the historical purist.

"I came to speak with all three of you. Are Janice and LuAnn gone?"

"No. They're in our apartment upstairs. I could call up and see if they're available."

Maybelline gave a quick nod. "If you don't mind."

Tess dialed LuAnn's number. "Maybelline is here," she said when her friend answered. "She wants to talk to all of us."

"Can you bring her up here so I don't have to leave Huck? We were gone most of the day."

"I'll ask. Taylor's still here to keep an eye on things."

She hung up and met Maybelline's gaze. "Do you mind if we go upstairs?"

At the hesitation in Maybelline's eyes, Tess hurried on. "Our dog was attacked by another dog yesterday, and LuAnn is keeping an eye on him."

"I don't mind." Her expression softened. "Poor thing. What happened?"

Tess stood and led her out of the office. While they rode the elevator to the fourth floor, Tess described the stray dog's attack on their little guy. Maybelline must have been a dog lover—or at least an animal lover—because her face remained fixed in sympathy. By the time they reached the apartment, she almost seemed like a normal person and not the buttoned-up, unpleasant woman they'd come to know. Maybe, for someone like Maybelline, all it took for her to soften was someone willing to give her the benefit of the doubt and befriend her.

They found Janice and LuAnn in the common living room, both with laps full of plastic eggs and a bag of candy. They greeted Maybelline, and Janice invited her to sit on the empty sofa.

"You two have gotten quite a few done," Tess said.

Janice rolled her eyes. "We have miles to go before we sleep."

Huck lay on his bed next to LuAnn's chair. He briefly raised his head to observe the new face in the room, then settled back down.

"How is he?" Tess asked, sitting at the other end of the sofa.

"Sleepy. The vet said to expect it for a few days while he heals. He's starting to go to the door again when he needs out, but I can't put the leash on him, because he can't wear a collar. One of the bites is on his neck."

"The poor thing," Maybelline said again, her gaze on Huck.

LuAnn popped an egg open. "At least he's staying close and not trying to run off."

"You know he was a stray when he found us," Janice said. "We all fell in love with him right away. Well...I mean..." She cast a guilty glance toward Tess.

Tess smiled sheepishly. "I was the holdout." Not because she had anything against dogs. "I had lost dogs I loved, and I wasn't sure I was ready to love another one. Now he's like part of the family."

"I can imagine," Maybelline said. "Animals keep away the loneliness."

Janice's eyebrows went up. "Do you have—?"

Maybelline cleared her throat and straightened her back on the sofa. "Let me get to the point." Clearly, she didn't want to discuss her personal life. Tess couldn't blame her, really. Had they ever tried to be her friend? They'd tried with Margaret Ashworth, maybe. Other than the museum and choir, Tess had no idea how Maybelline spent her time. Or who she spent it with.

"What can we do for you, Maybelline?" LuAnn said.

"I read the entry you mentioned in Prudence's journal, and I've looked into the matter of Jack O'Hara."

All three of the Inn Crowd leaned in.

"Of course I'd heard of Jack O'Hara from the Bickerton sisters, just like you, but I never really connected the dots. I mean, O'Hara isn't that uncommon a name, is it?"

It was for a town like Marietta. But none of them mentioned the fact. It wouldn't take much for their guest to clam up, and it seemed as though she might have more to say.

"I found a ledger that showed Jack O'Hara purchased five acres of land in 1859, and there's nothing that shows he ever sold it. I compared maps of Marietta from that time and now, and that land is exactly where the O'Hara mansion sits today."

"I wonder how Gibson O'Hara inherited the land," mused Tess.

"I've looked into that too," Maybelline said.

Janice smiled. "You planned for every question we could have."

"I suppose. I just followed my own thoughts."

"Well then," Janice said. "Great minds think alike."

An actual smile briefly broke out across Maybelline's face before she sobered. "Anyway, I found a document that showed the different owners for the land beginning with Jack. Jack had a sister, Roarke."

LuAnn nodded. "Go on."

"After the war, in 1870, the next owner was a man by the name of Miles Tennant. I'm sure you already know, women didn't own property back then, so I looked up marriage records. Miles Tennant married Roarke O'Hara that year. There is no bill of sale anywhere on file, so my guess is that Jack gave them the land for a wedding present."

Janice frowned. "But that still doesn't tell us what happened to Jack O'Hara."

A quick cloud passed over Maybelline's face, and her expression hardened. "I found what I could. It took quite a bit of time." She shot to her feet. "That's all I have for you. I need to go now."

"Wait," Janice said, moving so fast the eggs dropped to the floor. "Maybelline." She caught up with her at the door. "I'm sorry. The information you discovered about Jack's land is more than we could have ever found on our own. I wouldn't even have thought to look at maps or marriage records. I'm sorry if I sounded ungrateful."

Maybelline stopped, her hand on the doorknob. "I understand. But if you continue to look for answers about Jack O'Hara and his descendants, I hope you'll remember that whatever the O'Haras were or were not during the last century, Molly O'Hara will not be with us too many more years, her son is dead, and her grandson and great-grandson serve this town on the police and fire departments. It would be a kindness to allow them the choice about how much of their family history they want to reveal."

"We'll do our best," LuAnn said. "But it may not be our choice. Karl Mannus is pretty determined to find a connection to the mob."

She rolled her eyes. "Don't I know it. He's been in the museum every single day looking through old records and books."

"I'm surprised you let him."

"I guess I shouldn't admit this." She grinned, and Tess noticed a hint of a dimple in her right cheek. "But he promised to do a segment about the museum on his news show."

Janice laughed. "We can't blame you for wanting that."

"Besides, I don't think he'll find anything in those books. They're mostly genealogy."

Tess spoke up from her spot on the couch. "Why don't you stay and join us for supper, Maybelline? You'd be in for a treat. It's LuAnn's turn to cook, and I can see she has a lasagna sitting on the counter ready to go into the oven."

"Oh, you're right." LuAnn stood and walked toward the kitchen. "I better get it in the oven now."

Maybelline glanced from one to the other. "I don't want to put you out." There was an eagerness in her eyes that belied her words. "I mean, you weren't expecting company..."

"Don't be silly." Tess took her arm. "There's always a seat at our table for a friend."

"Okay, if you insist."

Janice grinned. "It's going to take that lasagna an hour to cook. How do your plastic-egg-filling skills measure up to your research skills?"

When Maybelline laughed out loud, it occurred to Tess that her particular laugh had likely not been heard in Marietta for a very long time, if ever. She smiled, determined to give Maybelline more reasons to laugh in the future.

Tuesday dawned with a beautiful sun shining in Tess's window. She smiled as she slowly came awake, then sat up suddenly. Sun! When was the last time she'd slept until after sunup? She glanced at the clock on her bedside table. The red numbers flashed twelve o'clock. Mercy, the power must have gone off sometime during the night. Lizzie was always telling her she should use a backup alarm on her phone. Well, from now on she would!

After supper last night they'd filled more eggs. Maybelline had remained to help, and they stayed up until after eleven while they worked and talked. Maybelline didn't open up too much, but she seemed to enjoy their stories of adventures they'd had during college. It had been a pleasant evening, and they'd filled almost all the eggs that were left.

But that was no excuse for Tess to oversleep while Winnie and Janice and LuAnn did all the work. She left the warmth of her bed and straightened the covers before pulling on her clothes and slipping into comfortable shoes.

She rushed out the door and down the stairs. When she reached the second floor, Titus was walking up the stairs holding tightly to the railing for support. "Good morning, Tess. I missed you at breakfast."

"I can't imagine why on earth they let me sleep in."

He smiled. "Sometimes good friends know when a person just needs a little extra rest."

"I'll blame the power outage. I wonder why it went out."

He grinned. "You must have really been out. The storm kicked up around one and was loud enough to rattle the building for a good hour."

Tess shook her head. "For goodness' sake. I had no idea." And she was usually such a light sleeper. "I better get down there and help out."

"Breakfast is almost over. Robin is just cleaning the café, and LuAnn and Janice are in the kitchen, I think." He made it to the second floor and stopped before taking the rest of the stairs to his room. "Will you and the other ladies have a few minutes this evening? You remember I said I had some exciting news for you—there's someone I'd like to introduce you to."

"I'm sure we will. Can you come up to the apartment around seven?"

He nodded. "You'll let me know if something comes up with one of the others?"

"Of course."

"I'll be leaving soon for an appointment, then I'll be going out for lunch, but I should be back around two. If you find it's not convenient, you can let me know then."

They parted ways, Titus to his room and Tess resuming her guilty walk to the kitchen. She entered to the sound of laughter and the dishwasher. Janice glanced up. "The lady of leisure has arrived."

"Don't tease her," Winnie scolded. Tess smiled at her. Their loyal friend and cook would defend any of them with the same intensity. "Sometimes a body just needs rest, and God works it out, even if He has to knock out manmade power to accomplish it."

"I feel refreshed, but guilty." Tess walked to the cabinet and got a cup and poured her morning coffee. "Why didn't you two wake me up?"

LuAnn and Janice exchanged a glance and smiled. "Because for the last couple of weeks you've been the first one up most days, and the last one to bed," LuAnn said.

Janice nodded. "We decided to let you sleep. And that's that."

"Thank you. And I'll return the favor sometime."

She filled them in on Titus's request while they joined her for a cup of coffee, and Winnie kneaded dough for lunch.

"The only plan I have," said Janice, "is filling more eggs. You know I dreamed about those crazy colors last night?"

LuAnn laughed. "Before or after the storm hit?"

"Both!"

"I don't have plans either," LuAnn said. "I wonder if he wants to introduce us to the woman we saw him talking to that night."

Tess was almost sure that would be the case. And she still hadn't filled them in on Titus's revelation to her. "I found out who the woman is. Sort of."

"What? How?" Janice asked.

"Yesterday, at breakfast, Titus told me he's been getting memories back a little at a time."

"Oh, gracious," Janice said. "Does he remember his wife? Or any children?"

"He didn't get that far, because Justin showed up in the fire truck before he could say much, and then everything was chaotic all day."

"Well," LuAnn said. "What *did* he say?"

"That the woman he met at the coffeehouse had apparently followed him there. Well, I'm not sure about that. But she approached him and called him *Mickey*."

Janice gasped. "Like Molly did."

Tess nodded. "Exactly. Apparently, he is a veterinarian from Morristown, New Jersey. The woman we saw evidently worked with him sometime in the past. She came all the way from New Jersey to find him."

LuAnn's eyebrows rose. "That's dedication."

Tess lifted her cup. "That's what I thought." She sipped her coffee then set it back down.

"What else did Titus say?" Janice asked.

Releasing a sigh, Tess shrugged. "Justin turned on his siren, and that was that."

"Okay," said Winnie. "It sounds like the mystery of Titus Jones is about to be solved without you three solving it this time."

LuAnn rested her chin in her palm. "Yeah."

Winnie put her hand on LuAnn's shoulder. "Don't look so disappointed. All of you. The Lord reveals His mysteries to whoever He chooses. And this time it wasn't you three."

"At any rate," Janice said, "at least we'll find out about his past."

Still, it didn't explain why Titus had changed his name. Nor did it explain the money and the locket. Even the newspaper articles were a conundrum. Why did Titus save them for so many years?

There was nothing to be done right now except go about the day as usual. But Tess had a feeling time was going to feel like it was standing still—like the flashing numbers on an alarm clock that never changed time.

CHAPTER SIXTEEN

May 19, 1863

"Stay in the wagon with Moses," Jason instructed as he pulled the reins to halt the horses. He set the brake and wrapped the reins around the lever.

Gideon sat in the back of the wagon with his arm around Brown. He was clearly trying to keep the dog calm as he stroked his fur. He looked up and saw Prudence and smiled.

"Is there a problem here?" Jason asked.

"This doesn't concern you," the Union captain said sharply. "Move along."

"The boy was taken from our home, Captain," Jason said. "We came to find him."

"Now look here, it's true, we took the boy from these fine folks' house," Jack O'Hara said. "But it wasn't like that. My sister and I were just looking after the tyke. We were trying to save him from going back to the life of a slave."

For the first time Prudence noticed there was a woman sitting on the wagon seat next to Jack. The couple of times she'd noticed the woman in town, she had assumed she was

Mrs. O'Hara. Now, she could see the resemblance between them. The back of the wagon was filled with crates and a couple of rocking chairs. It was clear they were lighting out and had no plans to return.

The captain barked an order to his men. They dismounted and started unloading the crates.

"Now, see here," O'Hara protested. "Those supplies were bought and paid for honestly. You don't have the right to—"

"We do have the right," the captain said. "Leave one crate of supplies and take the rest. Don't take their personal items." His gaze roved over Gideon. "Are you with this man and woman willingly?" he asked the boy.

Relief flooded Prudence. All he had to do was shake his head, and he'd be on his way back home with them. But to her shock, he smiled at the soldier and nodded.

"Gideon!"

"Ma'am, the boy obviously isn't under duress, and he's clearly not your child. So, unless you tell me he's your slave, and Mr. Lincoln says you can keep him since you're in a state loyal to the Union, I'll have no choice but to let him go."

"He most certainly is not our slave." But West Virginia, as they were tentatively calling the portion of Virginia loyal to the Union, was allowed to keep their slaves for now as well. The soldiers could easily send him back to the Wimber plantation if they were of a mind to.

"We are requisitioning these supplies, but you can work out between yourselves what to do about the boy."

They loaded the goods into a supply wagon. Jack hauled himself from the wagon and walked to her. "Now, Mrs. Willard," he said, "I'm sorry for the way I went about this. But I got tipped off that the army was coming to raid my barn and take all my goods." He scowled. "The dirty thieves."

Prudence leveled a questioning look at Jack. "Thee has not explained why Gideon is in thy wagon. Why did thee steal him from our home? Th-thee had no right." Her voice broke with tears, and her eyes stung.

"Mrs. Willard. Believe me when I say I didn't want to do things this way. I got word yesterday, at the Wimbers. Remember when I said I was being watched?"

Prudence nodded, the lump in her throat preventing a reply.

"I took supplies to Mrs. Wimber yesterday. She told me her men were going to be taking the boy from your place. She don't have many slaves helping her anymore, and she said a boy his age would be a big help." He glanced at Gideon, then back to Prudence. "I'm pretty sure she's the one that told the soldiers about my supplies. They're a bunch of thieves, stealing food right out of the mouths of decent folks to feed the army. I figured if all my supplies were going to be gone anyway, I might just as well grab the boy and take him with me, so that woman couldn't have him back."

Jason had been listening, and he looked at Prudence. She didn't want to hear what he had to say. "Pru," he said, softly, "Gideon told the captain he wants to go with Jack."

"Wh-where will thee take him?"

"Ma'am," he said, "we're heading back to New York. Our people are there. And my cousin Frank has work for me. The boy will be safe with me and my sister. We'll raise him up right."

Prudence turned her gaze to Gideon. He was staring at her, his eyes wide with hope. Clearly, he wanted to go with Jack. She fought back her tears.

Nevertheless, not my will but Thine be done.

"And what sort of work will thee be doing once thee gets to New York, Jack?" she asked.

"Oh, Frank has a couple of stores. Kelly and Sons. His boys are off fighting. He didn't want me to leave in the first place. I'll have to eat a little crow when I get back, but he'll take us in until we get on our feet."

She nodded, swallowing hard. She looked at Gideon again. "And this is what thee wants to do? Go with Jack?"

He nodded again.

"God go with thee all. Please send word when thee arrives safely. And perhaps from time to time, thee might keep me apprised of how Gideon is doing."

"Yes ma'am," he said, with uncommon gentleness. "And, ma'am? I'll always remember the things we talked about."

"Then, we shall pray for thy safe journey and for goodness and mercy to follow thee all the days of thy life."

Lunch was busy enough that time flew for the three hours the café was open. Tess stood in the kitchen dishing out chicken and dumplings when Robin burst into the kitchen, clearly shaken.

"Tess!" she said. "There's a man with a badge out there asking to see this man." Robin shoved a photograph toward her. "That's Titus Jones, right?" It was clearly Titus standing with a puppy... that looked an awful lot like a younger Huck. "He called him Mickey and said he's a missing person."

"Did you tell him Titus is staying here?"

Robin shook her head. "No, but I'm pretty sure he knows it."

"Are there a lot of customers?"

"No, just him and a couple others. The rest have gone."

"It's almost two." Tess's heart caught in her throat. Titus was supposed to be back around this time. "I'll take care of it if you can help Winnie and LuAnn for a little while. Is Janice in the dining room?"

"She's the one that seated the guy and waited on him, but there was a call a few minutes ago. She took it."

"Okay, I'll go talk to the officer. What does he have to drink?"

"Iced tea."

Grabbing the pitcher, Tess went into the café and walked to the table. She filled the policeman's glass, then set the pitcher on the table. She took the photo from her pocket and set it in front of him as well. "I'm Tess Wallace, one of the owners. Robin said you are asking about this man?"

"That's right." He pulled out his badge and handed it to her. Detective Kelly. Kelly?

Tess wasn't sure how to handle the situation. Should she reveal that she was aware of just what Kelly family he came from, or play dumb? As it turned out, the decision wasn't hers to make. He chuckled.

"I see you know the family name."

"We have a reporter staying with us who covered Molly O'Hara's birthday party. He's been connecting the dots between your two families for the last few days."

"Yeah, he's been hanging around my great-aunt's house trying to get a word with me."

That explained how Detective Kelly knew where to find Titus. Karl must've told him he'd seen Titus here.

She gave him back the badge. "You're a little out of your jurisdiction, aren't you?"

"I'm not arresting anyone." He grinned. "Just asking questions."

"I'm sorry, but we don't answer questions about our guests without a subpoena."

"Even if they're dangerous?" His piercing gaze sent a chill down her spine.

"If he's so dangerous, what did he do? And why aren't you involving the local police?"

"Obviously, I can't give out details about a suspect any more than you, apparently, can share information about your guests."

"Well, then—"

"You clearly know the man I'm looking for. And I can get the cooperation I need from my cousin. He's a sergeant in the police department in your little town. He definitely has jurisdiction."

"I happen to know Johnny and his wife pretty well. He won't try to bully me for answers."

"I certainly don't mean to bully you either, Ms. Wallace, was it? I hope you'll accept my apology if I've offended you." He stood, leaving half of his meal and dropping a nice tip for Robin. At least he had that much going for him. Tess followed him to the register, where she silently waited as he paid his bill. He set the photo of Titus on the counter. "You keep it. Show it to Mickey, and tell him I'll be seeing him soon."

Tess watched him leave, praying Titus didn't return while the detective was still on the premises. She breathed a sigh of relief when he drove away.

She picked up the photograph and stared at the man they'd all grown so fond of in such a short time. He looked like the same kind man they had come to know. It was very difficult for Tess to believe he could have ever been anything but good. But what if there really was someone dangerous hiding in his subconscious mind, just waiting for him to remember?

Janice entered the café just as Tess finished cleaning off the detective's table, and together they went to the kitchen to find LuAnn. Robin had already filled her in on the detective's presence and the photograph. Tess pulled it out of her pocket and handed it to Janice. "He's asking for Titus by the name of 'Mickey,' just like Molly did the other night. And look, he's holding Huck."

"It certainly looks that way," LuAnn said.

"So he's Titus's dog." Janice inhaled a heavy breath and exhaled. "That explains why such a good dog ended up a stray.

He must have jumped out of the car when it crashed and then ran away."

"I wonder if that explains why he was so scared being in my car and yours, Lu."

"I wouldn't doubt it. Do you think Titus remembers him?"

"Huck certainly seems taken with Titus." Tess shrugged. "Titus said he's starting to remember some things. So I suppose it's possible that Huck is one of those things."

They heard a huff and turned to find Winnie standing a few feet away, her hands on her hips. "Does this mean we have to give Huck back?"

Janice shook her head. "No. Finders keepers." She let out a sigh. "Unless he can provide proof of ownership, I guess."

Winnie gathered up a pile of dishtowels that had accumulated throughout the day. "I'm taking these to the washer," she said, her voice troubled.

Tess frowned. "Huck isn't microchipped. Doesn't it seem like a vet might have chipped his own dog?"

"We aren't really accomplishing anything by guessing about all of this," LuAnn said. "Let's make a list of the questions we want to ask and see if he's willing to answer them. But I definitely have to know his intentions about Huck. I don't know if I can…" Her voice broke, and she averted her gaze and sniffled.

Tess's eyes burned as tears started to form, and Janice already had a few tears sliding down her cheeks.

"Do you think," Janice said, her voice trembling as she spoke, "that God sent Huck to us so that we could take care of him until Titus was able to?"

LuAnn slid her arm around Janice's shoulders. "It's possible. It's also possible that we won't understand what God had in mind in all of this until we're standing in the middle of the answers."

Tess knew LuAnn was right. God's thoughts were higher, and He saw the end of a journey even when they were just taking the first or second or middle steps along the way.

"I suppose that's the wonder of living by faith," she said. "Trusting God to work things out in His timing."

LuAnn slid her arm from Janice's shoulder and took her hand. "The best thing we can do right now is pray." Tess completed the circle, and they bowed their heads.

The three ladies didn't have much of an appetite for dinner, so they just put together a few snacks, though Tess doubted she'd be able to eat a bite. She decided a diversion was needed. "Ladies, I think we should look at Prudence's diary again and see if we can find out any more about Jack O'Hara."

LuAnn stood up from the table. "I think that's a great idea. Janice, if you'll get the copies of the journal for us, I'll put the kettle on."

Tess took her journal from Janice and found the spot where they'd left off. "I'll skim to see if I see Jack's name again." She ran her eyes over the pages—familiar, she knew, to LuAnn, but not so much to herself. "Here's something. 'November 2, 1863. We received a letter from Jack today, telling us of Gideon's schooling and how well he's doing. Jack is a better man than he believes himself to be, and I know that Gideon is safe with him. My heart almost broke when they left here months ago, but I am filled with joy when I think of the opportunities that lie in Gideon's future. Jack says the entire O'Hara family has taken the boy under their wing and dote on him as if he were one of their own. Truly, if he is to be our last "package," God has answered my prayers above and beyond what I ever expected or imagined.'"

"That lets us know that Jack left Marietta," said LuAnn as she poured the tea. "I don't remember reading any more about Gideon—but then I didn't remember that she'd mentioned a Jack either." She chuckled. "You all will think twice before you rely on my historian's memory again."

Tess put down the diary and took her mug from LuAnn. "That's what your clues notebook is for, my dear Watson. After we eat, let's get it out and review. I have a feeling we're going to get to the bottom of this before too much longer."

Although Titus had said he'd return by two, he still hadn't returned to the inn when the three of them left the counter in Taylor's capable hands that evening and went upstairs. As the clock drew nearer to seven, Tess was beginning to worry that something had happened to him. Had Detective Kelly convinced Johnny to arrest him, or at the very least take him in for questioning? Was poor Titus at this moment sitting in a hard chair in awful pain because of his leg, being questioned about the locket missing from the O'Haras' or the money in his bag, if he had in fact stolen it?

Just as her imagination had convinced her of those things, there was a knock on the door. They all stood. "Whatever we discover," Tess said, "we've already asked for wisdom to know if we should contact the authorities or not. We asked for discernment so we can tell the truth from a lie. So here we go."

She opened the door to find Titus and the woman they had seen with him at the coffeehouse—a pretty, dark-haired woman of about forty with green eyes and skin the color of coffee with cream. She was beautiful. She stepped inside after Titus, and there was an air of confidence about her that felt a little intimidating. But she smiled as Tess closed the door. "Your inn is really very pretty."

"Thank you," all three of them said together.

An oversized purse hung from the woman's shoulder. Tess would have offered to put it on the coatrack for her, but she clung to it as though it was a lifeline and she was drowning.

"Please come this way," LuAnn said, motioning toward their sitting area. "We thought you would be more comfortable in the living room."

"Thank you, ladies," Titus said. "That was thoughtful." He leaned his cane against the end of the couch. "Farrah, these lovely ladies are LuAnn, Tess, and Janice, the owners of this magnificent inn. And ladies, let me introduce you to Farrah Truitt, my daughter."

Tess sucked in a breath at this news. That answered the question he had about whether or not he had children. And if

Farrah had come all this way to find him, then clearly his fears about not being a good enough father for his children were also put to rest. At least it appeared so.

"It's so nice to meet you," LuAnn said. "Let's sit down. Can I get you anything? Coffee? Tea?"

They both declined, and everyone took a seat. Tess looked at Titus. "Titus, while you were gone today, a man came into the café for lunch." She hesitated as all eyes turned to her. "He showed us a photo of you—after he showed us a New York police badge."

Farrah's jaw dropped a little, and she turned to look at her father. "Anson..."

Tess nodded. "Detective Kelly. I didn't hear his first name, but I suspected that's who he was. He said you were wanted because of something criminal but didn't elaborate."

A dark cloud passed over Farrah's features. "He's trying to frame you, Dad."

Titus nodded. "It would seem that way."

LuAnn had picked up the photo earlier and put it inside her notebook while they brainstormed questions they hoped Titus would address. She handed it to him now. "This is the photograph he showed us. He told Tess we should keep it and show it to you."

Farrah looked at the photo as Titus held it. "Dad, if Anson is here..."

Titus handed the photo back to LuAnn. "I suppose you ladies deserve an explanation."

"Only if you want to tell us."

He gathered a full breath and exhaled. "I've brought trouble to your door."

"But that isn't your fault, Dad," Farrah said, placing her hand on his forearm. "You can't help that you had the accident."

He smiled at her and covered her hand with his. "Be that as it may, trouble is here because of me." He slid his gaze from Tess to Janice, then LuAnn. "As you've probably guessed by now, Molly O'Hara was right. My name is Mickey Truitt, and I did know her sister, Francine…Figgy." He smiled. "I knew her my entire life, actually."

Tess's heart flipped. Would he explain the locket and the suitcase full of money? If he did, would that prove he was the good man they believed him to be, or the man Detective Kelly implied he was? "So your memory has returned?"

He nodded. "Every bit of it."

"That has to be a relief," Janice said softly.

He gave them a wry smile. "It's a mixed blessing."

Farrah squeezed his arm. "But it's better to know the truth."

"It's definitely better to remember you."

She laid her head on his shoulder as though she were a little girl. The gesture shot straight to Tess's heart. "But it must have been so difficult for you, Farrah," she said, "to lose your mother and then your father like that…" She didn't know if she should continue, but surely, they were all thinking of how hard it must have been for the young woman.

Farrah lifted her head. "What? My mother? My mother passed away in her sleep fifteen years ago."

"Yes, Tess," Mickey said. "I'm wondering where you got the idea that it was my wife I was coming to mourn. Can you remember what I said to you during our initial conversation last year?"

Tess's head was reeling. "Y-you said that someone close to you had died, and you needed to get away to mourn her passing. I just assumed you meant your wife."

Mickey bowed his head, and his shoulders shook. When he looked up, he was smiling. He must have seen Tess's expression, because he wiped his hand over his face and took a deep breath. "I'm sorry, Tess," he said. "I'm not laughing at your expense. Margie has been gone a long time, and I do still miss her, but that grief is far from fresh. It was Figgy who had passed away. I still need to mourn her death. Because of my amnesia, it seems to me as if she died very recently."

Farrah took his arm again. "The email with a photo of my father, taken right here at this inn, came so suddenly after all the months he was missing, I couldn't believe it."

"Do you know who sent you the email?"

"Yes. It was a man named Karl Mannus, and he said he was a reporter with Channel 8 news. He asked me all kinds of questions about the Kellys and O'Haras, so he must have found out something that linked Dad to them."

"I think he means well," Tess said. "But he's like a dog with a bone when he's onto something. Maybelline told us Karl has been going over ledgers and town records at the historical society. He also interviewed the Bickerton ladies and Molly O'Hara. There's no telling what sort of information he uncovered."

"We have experience deflecting questions from reporters," Farrah said with a wry smile.

At her words, Mickey seemed to take his cue. "My family has been connected with the Kellys and O'Haras for several generations." He leaned forward, resting his elbows on his knees and clasping his hands together in front of him. "I guess I should start at the very beginning. Jack O'Hara and Gilbert Kelly were cousins. Their parents came over from Ireland together early in the 1800s.

"Gilbert Kelly wasn't exactly a pillar of the community. He, along with a number of second-generation Irish immigrants, became frustrated with the poverty. America was supposed to be their salvation, but it didn't turn out that way. Not for them, at least. Jack O'Hara joined Gilbert, and together they ran a gang. Petty thievery, mostly. But it was violent and dangerous."

"And criminal," Janice said.

"Most definitely." Mickey nodded. "That's why Jack gave it up. When his mother was dying, he made her a promise that he would go straight. And he kept his promise. He took his cut of their enterprise and bought a team of horses and a wagon. They didn't have a definite destination in mind when they left New York. They thought maybe Oregon, but it was a long and dangerous trip, particularly traveling alone and not with a wagon train. But that's what they did. Just set out on their own and headed west. A few weeks into the journey, they met a fellow traveler who told them about a town he'd come from in Ohio."

"So that's how Jack ended up here?" LuAnn said. "He just thought Marietta sounded like as good a town as any to settle in?"

Mickey chuckled. "Not a very romantic tale, is it?"

"Oh, I don't know," Janice said. "To just turn your wagon west and start traveling. It's as romantic as any other story about the pioneers. I like it."

"So," Mickey continued, "Jack settled here in Marietta during the Civil War and mostly made his living by selling Union goods to the Confederacy. He was in Ohio for less than a year, but what happened in that year is what links his family and mine."

Tess looked at LuAnn and Janice. Both women were sitting forward in their seats, hanging on Mickey's every word. She knew they were thinking of the entry they'd read from Prudence's journal. "Would this have to do with a boy named Gideon?" she asked him.

He looked at her, his eyes wide. "You know about him?"

"We know that he left Marietta with Jack O'Hara sometime in the summer of 1863," Tess explained. "We don't know any more than that, except that the O'Hara family essentially adopted him as one of their own."

"Yes, that's right," said Mickey. "Both the Kellys and the O'Haras and their descendants maintained close ties with Gideon, his children and grandchildren, and so on down through the years. I'm a direct descendant of Gideon O'Hara. I never knew my father, and my mother died of breast cancer when I was ten. The Kellys took me in because of the close association of our families. Figgy was like a mother to me, and Nolan was the father I'd never had. Anson, their grandson, came along five or six years later, and he was like a younger brother to me.

We were close until he decided to take up the family business. By then I had finished college and married my wife. He was barely twenty, and I was in my thirties with a baby and a business to run. I didn't pay too much attention. I wish I had."

"But he's a detective," Janice said. "I'm confused."

"Let's just say he's not an honest detective. The gang kept police officers on the force to deflect from their criminal activities, and I always suspected that's why he joined in the first place. He did a very good job for the family."

"There's been speculation about Johnny O'Hara doing the same thing," Janice said. "But I've never really believed it."

"I wouldn't know. But considering the O'Haras left the business and moved to Marietta, I highly doubt that to be the case."

Relief washed over Tess.

"Anson had heard all the stories of the so-called glory days when the Kellys were flush with power. His father, Lyle, was arrested in the seventies and died in prison a few years later. Anson was only five or six when his mother left him, so it was Figgy and Nolan who raised him. Nolan was the one who filled his head with those stories, reliving his days as head of the Irish gang. He never stopped being involved in illegal practices, but after the gang crackdown in the sixties, they had to be sneakier about it. I think Figgy would have left Nolan if she hadn't been raising Lyle and then their grandson and me."

"Mickey, would you be willing to tell us why you left New York with an assumed identity?" Tess asked. She was glad to solve the mystery of Jack O'Hara, but Detective Kelly wasn't in Marietta looking for Jack—he was looking for Mickey.

"Dad, just tell them."

Janice leaned forward. "Tell us and let us help, if we can."

Mickey hesitated as though having a debate within himself.

"Would it help if we tell you what we already know?"

His eyebrows rose. "I suppose it might."

Tess thought back to the list of questions they'd written out earlier. "Last week I had to take my car in to be fixed. LuAnn and I were in the office when Dane, one of the mechanics, brought in your black vet bag. He spilled the beans about the contents of your suitcases."

Mickey nodded. "I was shocked when I saw that one bag was completely filled with money."

Farrah leaned in. "Dad sold his half of the business to me. We're both veterinarians."

Janice pressed her hand to her chest. "I'm so relieved. We just couldn't imagine why you had all that money and it was hard not to—"

"Wonder if he robbed a bank?" Farrah smiled.

"We didn't really believe he was a criminal."

Tess was as relieved as Janice to know Mickey had come by the money honestly, but she wanted to keep the answers coming. "That explains where the money came from. But there's something else we discovered when I went back to Ed's to get my car on Saturday. He showed us some news articles he'd found in your car wedged in the back seat. And when I came into your room for your medical bag, I saw the one about Molly's locket."

"And now it's missing."

"Yes."

"Let me see if I can explain. Twenty years ago, there was an up-and-coming senator whose campaign the Kelly family helped fund."

"Senator Craig Railey," Tess said.

Mickey expelled a sigh. "The senator was young and single, and my girl caught his eye."

"It was so much more than that," Farrah murmured.

"It was. The two of them fell in love after meeting at a function during his campaign. The problem was, Anson had been after Farrah for years, despite the fact that he is a good number of years older than she is. After Craig Railey was elected, he proposed to Farrah. Figgy threw an engagement party for them. Anson was drunk most of the night, becoming more and more combative."

"Craig drove me home," Farrah said. "When we got there Anson called and said he needed to speak with Craig right away. Craig tried to put him off until the next day, but Anson insisted, so finally he agreed to meet. I never saw Craig again. I confronted Anson, and he said Craig never showed up. Of course we found out later that he was lying, but he was on the police force and had made a name for himself. No one would believe my word over his."

Mickey took up the story. "Figgy confessed to me on her deathbed that Anson had killed Railey. She swore me to secrecy. What else could I do? She was dying. She told me she'd taken care of things, and I didn't have to worry."

His eyes flashed. "Then came the reading of the will. You have to understand, Figgy was the last one. The last of the great

Kellys and O'Haras. Everyone knew the family power would die with her. How much money she had and who she'd leave it to was fodder for the tabloids for at least four or five months before she died. But only Anson and I were allowed into the lawyer's office. When the will was read, both of us were stunned. Figgy had left all of her money and properties to me. She left Anson one dollar. One. What the lawyer read next let Anson know the reason."

Mickey took a deep breath. "Figgy talked of a great wrong that had been done twenty years before… Of a murder that had broken her beloved granddaughter's heart. And then she said she was leaving her mother's platinum locket to her sister, Molly O'Hara. Inside the locket, she said, she'd placed a slip of paper with the name of the murderer on it."

"But wait." Tess held up her hand. "I remember when Willa told me about the locket being stolen, she said that Molly had received it a couple of weeks ago. Why did it take so long for her to get it, if Figgy passed away last Thanksgiving?"

"Everything was delayed for legal reasons that I don't understand," said Mickey, "but I don't think it was unusual." He waved his hand. "So, anyway, when I heard that, I decided to come to Marietta under a false identity and talk to Molly, Johnny, and Willa about the locket and what they would find inside. But, as you know, I had an accident, and here I am."

Farrah looked at the ladies, her eyes wet with tears. "And he's been here, by himself, for over four months, not remembering who he is, not knowing he had loved ones desperate to find him. We had no idea he'd come to Marietta. We just knew he'd sold his half of the business and left."

Mickey put his arm around her. "I knew I couldn't tell Farrah. The less she knew the safer she would be. I didn't believe Anson would ever harm her. He'd been in love with her for more than twenty years. I planned to make a deal with the FBI for her protection, but the accident happened and then the amnesia. And now Anson has come to Marietta because he knows the locket has been delivered to Molly. I would bet everything I inherited from Figgy that he's been in town for a few days and was the one who stole that locket. I don't even know if the Marietta O'Haras have ever met him, so he could have easily crashed the party, especially with there being so many unexpected extra guests."

"So that explains why you have all those newspaper clippings," said LuAnn. "But there's still something I don't understand. Why hasn't Willa or Johnny told the police about the slip of paper in the locket? Why is Anson running around Marietta free as a bird?"

"I think I know the answer to that," said Tess. "Willa told me that Molly put the locket on when it came and hadn't taken it off until it was stolen Friday night. I would guess that no one but Molly knows what's in that locket, if even she does."

"Titus," Janice said. "Or rather, Mickey, I guess, we have a friend in the FBI. He's helped us out a couple of times. I could call him."

"A few days ago, I would've welcomed that course of action," Mickey said. "But with my daughter and Anson both in town, I can't risk putting her in danger."

"And I can't put him in danger either," Farrah said. "I never thought Anson was capable of murder. I honestly believed Anson when he said Craig didn't show up that night. I didn't know the truth until Dad told me today."

"We're leaving town tonight," Mickey said.

"Do you think Anson might be watching the inn for you?" Tess asked.

"I'm sure he is. Or will be." Mickey stood. "I took my bags to Farrah's hotel last night. Before we leave, she's going to call Anson and suggest they meet somewhere away from the inn. Which he will agree to. Then we'll drive in the opposite direction."

The idea wasn't foolproof, but Tess supposed it was the only option they had.

Farrah stood alongside her father. "Thank you for being so good to my dad."

Janice stepped forward and gave her a hug. "You two let us know when you're safe."

"We will."

"We'll walk you out."

Mickey shook his head. "As much as I'd like that, we need to look as normal as possible. Not like we're leaving. Just in case Anson has someone watching the inn."

"Then we'll say our goodbyes here." LuAnn walked to Mickey and took his arm as they went to the door.

"There is one more thing."

LuAnn smiled. "Huck."

He nodded. "He was Figgy's dog, and she loved him more than anything in the world."

Tess smirked. "I'm guessing his name is Capone."

"Yes. Figgy asked me to take him so he'd be treated well. He was with me when I had the accident. I guess he jumped out when I crashed and the door flew open. You ladies saved him by taking him in."

"You— Do you want him back?" Janice asked.

"I think he's found his home. We don't know where we'll end up or what road we'll take to get there. If you're willing, I'd appreciate it if you'd keep him."

Relief moved across LuAnn's face. "We will definitely do that."

"Mickey," Tess said. "I know you don't want us involved, but my friend with the FBI is Charles Butler. He's in the Canton field office. If you do go that way, you can tell him your story. He'll believe you."

"Charles Butler. Canton." Mickey nodded. "I'll keep it in mind."

A minute later, they were gone. LuAnn, Tess, and Janice walked soberly to the living room. "You know what we need to do now?" LuAnn asked.

Tess nodded. "Pray."

***

There was no sign of Anson Kelly for the next few days as Tess and her friends tended the inn and worked toward the upcoming Easter EGGstravaganza. Karl had made himself scarce but hadn't checked out. They caught glimpses of him here and there and could only guess that he was working on his story and didn't want to be bothered.

One person they did see often was Maybelline. She had worked tirelessly to help set up the grounds and suggested a tradition she had discovered in her studies, of the children flying kites to symbolize Jesus's ascension. She had organized the choir and the youth group from church, and they'd made several hundred small kites to pass out to the children. She was like a different person.

On Friday night, the Inn Crowd sat in the living room of their apartment drinking decaf tea. It was after eleven, and they were exhausted but satisfied that everything was ready for the next day.

"It'll be worth it," Tess said. "All the happy kids."

Janice beamed, and her eyes were soft and dreamy. "Lawrence and I always hosted an egg hunt for the children at Christ Fellowship. But it was never anything like this one is shaping up to be. I never even thought about face painting and a booth for making friendship bracelets. The children of our community will love it."

LuAnn nodded. "As well as Maybelline's kite idea."

"She's been a wonder, getting that organized so quickly," Tess said.

"What I love the most about it," Janice said, "is the chance to bring in the true meaning of Easter without hitting anyone over the head. The kids will have fun while they're learning about what Jesus did for us."

"Agreed," Tess said.

LuAnn yawned. "We better get some sleep." She stood and carried her teacup to the sink. "I'm heading to bed."

Tess and Janice followed suit.

***

The morning of the Easter EGGstravaganza couldn't have been more perfect. The temperature was projected to be close to seventy degrees in the afternoon, and the sun was bright.

Though the festivities were scheduled to start at noon, by eleven thirty the grounds were already flooded with people. As they had expected, hundreds of children waited with their baskets. Tess was excited that Lizzie and Michael had brought the triplets, and Janice was beaming as Stacy and Larry arrived, accompanied by Stuart. And as he'd promised, Karl showed up with a camera in tow to cover the whole thing.

Tess was thrilled to see who was behind the camera, but it was well after two o'clock before she had the chance to welcome her. "Shyla! You're back."

"I had the weekend off, so I couldn't resist. This is exciting!" She smiled, her eyes shining with joy. "Besides, I missed my husband."

"We haven't seen much of Karl the past few days either."

"He says he has almost everything he needs for the story. We're hoping it'll get that station in New York interested enough to make an offer."

Tess was curious what he'd discovered, but there wasn't a lot of time to dwell on it. Henry ran to her and grabbed her hand. "Mimi, will you play with me?"

"Of course I will. Where are we going?"

"The bouncy house."

She did a quick check to make sure he was wearing his wristband that matched Lizzie's and Michael's.

Turning back to Shyla, she shrugged. "My grandson wants me to play with him."

Shyla laughed. "I'll see you later."

Tess had just made her way out of the bouncy house maze with Henry when she spotted Charles and Rebekah Butler and their twins standing in line at the face painting booth. Henry ran to his mother, and Tess went to say hello. "You made it," she said.

"We've been here for some time," Rebekah said. "You all have done a fantastic job. It's like a fair. The kids are having a blast."

"Did they make it here in time for their age group's Easter egg hunt?"

"Oh, yes. Observe." Charles held up two baskets filled with eggs.

Tess laughed. "Make sure they look inside them. Some of them have tickets. There's a prize booth as you leave, and they can go in there and trade their tickets for different prizes. Some of the donations are pretty nice."

"Will do. Did you ever solve the mystery of your missing person?"

"We did. There was a guest staying here with amnesia, and we couldn't find any information on him. But he regained his memory and left the inn earlier this week."

"So everything was resolved then."

"For the most part."

Charles's eyes clouded with curiosity, but Tess didn't want to go into the issue of the locket and Anson Kelly. "Look, it's your kids' turn to get their faces painted. I'll talk to you later."

Tess continued her walk around the grounds, picking up fallen wrappers and other trash and offering her help at various booths, until she passed the kite booth around four. Maybelline had stayed there all day without taking a break, so Tess offered to take her place. But Maybelline shook her head. "Look at those kites flying. With each new group of kids, I have the honor of proclaiming the gospel. I'm reminded over and over of the awesome privilege it is to know Him." Her eyes shone with excitement and joy.

Her enthusiasm was catching, and as Tess walked around, she noted many of the children holding tightly to their kites.

Just before closing, she joined Janice, who was handing out cotton candy close to the exit. "Tess!" Janice said. "I'm so glad to see you."

"What's wrong?"

"I saw Anson Kelly a little while ago."

"Where?"

"Over there." She jerked her head to where Tess's son-in-law, Michael, had posed for photos as the Easter Bunny.

"Are you sure?" Tess asked. "I assumed he'd left town."

"I'm as sure as I can be. But I don't see him now."

"We'll keep an eye out. Maybe he came with Justin to help with the fire truck or something."

They ran out of cotton candy right before five o'clock. Janice went to find LuAnn, and Stuart announced from the loudspeaker they would be closing things down. The advertisements had said five o'clock, and it was ten minutes until five. As much fun as the day had been, Tess was more than ready to tidy up and relax after the event.

"Mom." Tess turned to find Lizzie standing with the triplets. "Have you seen Michael?"

"He was talking to Karl Mannus earlier. In full costume." Tess grinned. The children didn't know the Easter Bunny was actually their daddy, and they had been just as excited to sit and have their photographs taken as the other young children.

"I haven't seen either of them in some time."

"I'm sure he just decided to get out of that hot costume. He was a good sport, staying in that thing for as many hours as he did."

"I suppose. But I'm going to let the triplets have one more run at a couple of the bouncy houses before they take them down, and then I need Michael to look after them so I can get the birthday party stuff ready in the kitchen."

"I'll go look for him while you take the kids to play a little more."

Everything was quiet when Tess walked inside the inn. They had locked the doors and asked guests to use their keys to get inside during the festivities so they didn't chance a lot of traffic from those who came for the Easter EGGstravaganza. She heard voices in the living room and smiled. Maybe the men had hidden away in there. But it was Janice and LuAnn, sitting with their feet up.

"There you are," LuAnn said. "We wondered if you were setting up for the triplets' party already." Lizzie and Michael had decided they would kill two birds with one stone and have the kids' birthday party right after the egg hunt, since they'd been partying all afternoon anyway.

Tess waved her hand. "I'm actually looking for a certain Easter Bunny. He's gone conveniently missing."

"Oh, I saw him getting into Karl's car a little while ago."

"You did?"

"No, you didn't."

Tess turned to find Michael leaning against the doorframe. His hair was disheveled, and he wore a pair of basketball shorts and a T-shirt. He was holding on to the back of his head.

"Michael!" Tess said. "What happened?"

"A guy with a gun." He shook his head. "He followed me inside earlier and forced me to take off the suit. Then he must have knocked me out."

Tess took his arm and led him to the couch. "Janice, will you call Stuart and ask him to come in and check Michael out? He's still outside with Stacy and Larry."

Janice pulled out her phone. "Stuart, we need you in the house. We're in the sitting room on the first floor."

LuAnn pulled her shoes back on. "We need to call the police. It seems like Anson kidnapped Karl."

"Wait," Tess said. "Don't do that. What if…"

"What, Tess?" Janice asked.

"We know Johnny pretty well. But Anson is a police officer too, and he's not an honest one. What if we call the police and Johnny's part of the problem?"

"What trouble have you three gotten yourselves into this time?" Michael asked, leaning back against the couch.

"Let us worry about that," Tess said.

Janice nodded. "And don't go to sleep. You might have a concussion."

LuAnn stood. "Where's Agent Butler? This is a federal matter anyway. We know we can trust him."

Lizzie and Stuart entered the living room together.

"There you are," Lizzie said to Michael. "Stacy took Larry and the triplets up to the apartment to get them cleaned up."

"What did you need me for?" Stuart asked.

Michael raised his hand.

As Lizzie rushed to her husband and Stuart looked at his head, Tess, Janice, and LuAnn left the room as quietly as possible. Shyla met them in the foyer. "Have you seen Karl?"

"He left a few minutes ago," LuAnn said.

"Left? Do you know where he went?"

"No."

"He's not answering his phone. We're supposed to leave tonight, and he hasn't packed yet." She shook her head. "I guess I'll go up to his room and pack for him."

"Good idea," Tess said. "Do you need the key?"

"I already have it."

Tess went to the office and grabbed her purse, and then they slipped out of the inn and piled into her car. "Call Charles," Tess said to Janice. "Tell him we think Anson kidnapped Karl and we're going to the O'Hara mansion to find out."

Janice grabbed her cell phone and called his number but ended up leaving a voice mail. "He didn't pick up."

"What if he took him to a warehouse or something?" Janice asked. "We'd be wasting valuable time."

"Anson stayed at the O'Haras, and only Molly lives there with her nurse. As big as that house is, he could easily hide a kidnap victim."

"Why do you think he stole the Easter Bunny costume?" LuAnn asked.

"Probably so he could move around the grounds while he looked for Karl," Janice said. "I'm sure he knew I saw him earlier."

"That makes sense."

"Hurry, but don't speed," LuAnn urged her. "There's no telling how long of a head start he has."

They parked by the side of the road, a block from the O'Haras' mansion, and walked the rest of the way. "Look," Janice said. "Anson didn't even try to hide Karl's car."

Sure enough, Karl's car sat in the driveway, bold as you please. The ladies snuck up to the living room window and peeked inside. "Look," Janice whispered. "There he is."

They could only see the back of Karl's head as he sat in a wing chair facing away from the window. But Anson paced the room, a gun in his hand.

"What are you three doing here?" A whispered voice behind them made them jump.

They turned to find Agent Butler. "What are *you* doing here?" Janice asked. "I just called you a few minutes ago."

"Your kids told me you disappeared after Michael was assaulted. So of course I followed you." His face grew stern. "Now tell me, what are *you* doing here?"

"We're saving Karl. That man with the gun kidnapped him."

"Ladies, it's too dangerous. Go home."

He went to the front door and checked it. Then he turned the knob and went in with his gun drawn.

"Should we follow him?" Janice asked, wide-eyed.

"Probably not." LuAnn said.

They waited for a few minutes.

"Don't you think Charles will protect us?" Janice asked.

"Yes, but do we want to divide his focus?" Tess said.

"I have an idea," LuAnn said. "If we go around to the patio entrance, we can get inside. There are more places to hide in the back of the house, and it's farther from the living room than the front door."

Tess liked that idea better than barging in through the front door. "What if it's locked?"

"It's worth a try," LuAnn said. "Besides, Willa told me as much as they try to keep it locked, Molly wanders out there a lot."

"Bless her heart," Janice said. "She probably does have fond memories of the garden parties they used to have."

"Okay," Tess said. "Let's go."

They made their way around the enormous house and onto the patio. They peeked inside the glass doors and found the foyer empty. LuAnn reached out and tested the door. "It's unlocked."

They slowly opened the door and filed in. They flattened themselves against the wall as they took stealthy side steps, following the sound of the voices, toward the living room.

They stopped right outside the door. Anson was speaking. "So, my grams sent the locket here to Aunt Molly." He sighed. "I had to get that paper before Johnny saw it. I came as soon as the lawyer let me know it had been sent. I'm telling you, it was an accident." Tess ventured a peek around the door and almost gasped. Karl was taking notes. She turned to Janice and LuAnn. "Look in there." She stepped aside so they could.

"Goodness gracious goat," Janice whispered. "Karl got his interview."

"Let's hope he doesn't get whacked."

"Where's Agent Butler?"

"I'm here."

They turned at the sound of the whisper to find Agent Butler crouched behind a large curio cabinet just next to the door. He gave them an exasperated glare. "Didn't I tell you to go home?"

Tess had opened her mouth to reply when, with his gun drawn, Charles stepped out into the living room. "FBI. No one move."

CHAPTER SEVENTEEN

The fourth birthday party for the triplets went off famously. After "Happy Birthday" had been sung, the cake eaten and cleaned up, the presents opened, and everyone had gone home, LuAnn, Tess, and Janice sat, exhausted, in their apartment. LuAnn was writing in her notebook to put the ending on yet another mystery solved. "So, Figgy told Mickey that Anson murdered that senator, and that's why all this happened," she said.

Tess nodded. "Like he told us, the reason he came to Marietta was because Figgy gave him a deathbed confession about Anson killing the senator. All these years, she's believed her son murdered him. But Anson says that during his meeting with Railey, the senator saw an antique gun and was curious about it. Anson showed it to him—and this is the senseless part—when they were fooling with it, it went off and killed Railey."

"You'd think they'd have just called the police." LuAnn said, shaking her head. "That's what innocent people do."

"Except," Janice said, "who would believe anything like that if it involved a mafia family? And don't forget, Anson had the motive of being in love with the victim's fiancée."

"So Mickey drove here with all that cash and a fake identity?"

Tess nodded. "Figgy wanted the truth to come out so the senator's family could put it to rest, but she didn't want it to happen until she was gone. Mickey told Karl everything he believed before he left with Farrah. Anson saw them together and wanted to know what Mickey had told him. I guess a mobster doesn't go to the trouble of making an appointment. They just whack a giant Easter bunny on the head and kidnap the informant. Anson wanted his version of the story to get out, and that's what he needed Karl for."

Janice shook her head. "So, Karl finally has his big story, and Molly got her locket back."

"Looks that way." Tess couldn't help but laugh. "Karl's getting everything he wanted. Apparently two national news outlets are interested in the story. And him. So he got an even better offer than he was hoping for."

LuAnn brushed her hands together. "Well, ladies. I guess that's that."

The buzzer went off, signaling that someone had come to the door downstairs. "After ten o'clock?"

"I'll go," Tess said. "Since I'm the only one still dressed."

"We'll all go," Janice said. "Who knows who it could be? We'll take Huck with us, though, just in case we need reinforcements." She laughed and opened the door, calling for Huck.

They went down the stairs together and walked abreast to the door. Tess reached out and twisted the lock, then the knob.

A familiar figure stood on the porch, his bags next to him. In his arms, he held a pot of forget-me-nots. Huck wiggled all over, and Tess picked him up to keep him from climbing

Mickey's legs. "We received a call from Charles Butler," he said. "Apparently, there is no need for me to rush off. I wonder if you might have a room for me."

"Of course," Janice said. "Come in, Titus. Oh, I suppose that's Mickey now, isn't it?"

"Where's Farrah?" Tess asked.

"She left for New Jersey. She does have a veterinary practice to run, and now that Anson has been arrested, there's nothing for her to fear."

Janice smiled and took one of his bags. "We saved Karl tonight. Well, we didn't really *save* him, but we almost did, I mean, we would have, if he'd been in any danger..."

Mickey Truitt glanced over his shoulder and smiled with affection as Janice rattled on.

LuAnn grinned, watching Mickey and Janice walk off together. "I think that's the beginning of a beautiful friendship."

Gratitude swelled inside Tess as she watched her friends get Mickey checked in. She was suddenly struck with the thought that sometimes God sends a "stray" into His children's lives when they least expect it. He'd brought Gideon into Prudence's life. And He'd brought Mickey into her life, and Huck, and even little Tom. She thought of how long it had taken her to accept Huck's doggie love when he first came. God certainly knew best. All of her strays had ended up blessing her far more than she could ever hope to bless them.

Tess hugged Huck a little tighter and kissed the top of his head. "Come on, little fellow, let's get upstairs. You're sleeping in my room tonight."

Dear Reader,

The ladies of Wayfarers Inn inspire me. They take in the broken and go out of their way to make a difference. Can you imagine owning an inn where every guest is an opportunity to show the love of God?...Even guests like Titus, who came to them broken in body, yes, but more than that, broken in spirit, not knowing who he was. Was he good or evil? Did the people he'd left behind in his former world mourn that he was missing, or did his absence make their lives better? Would it be better for him to rebuild his life from the ground up rather than risk finding out he wasn't the man he wanted to be?

The good thing about living this Christian life is that God lets us reinvent ourselves as much as we are willing to change. At nearly fifty years old, I'm still making mistakes, still learning from them, and still pressing on to know Jesus and be changed into His image.

I truly hope you enjoy *Forget-Me-Nots*. Thank you for, once again, hanging out with me in Marietta.

Signed,
Tracey Bateman

ABOUT THE AUTHOR

Tracey Bateman writes from the beautiful Missouri Ozarks, where there is much scope for the imagination. With four grown children and four grandchildren, she and her husband are filled with the wonder of God's goodness. They are enjoying empty nesting and watching their growing family live, love, laugh, and thrive.

The Castle

RESIDENCE OF JOHN NEWTON ESQ. FOURTH ST. MARIETTA, OHIO.

The Castle was the home of some of Marietta's most prominent and influential citizens. The property was leased as early as 1808 by a potter and his family, making it one of the earliest pottery manufacturing sites in the entire Northwest Territory. The Gothic Revival house was built in 1855, and a carriage house was completed just three years later. The Castle hosted a number of grand functions throughout its history. Only five families have lived on the property between 1808 and 1974. These residents included lawyers, bankers, land and oil speculators, and a President Pro Tem of the Ohio Senate.

Upon the death of its last resident, Jessie (Davis) Lindsay, the property was purchased at auction by Bertlyn and Stewart Bosley in 1974. The brother and sister spent the next seventeen years renovating and restoring the house, but never resided at the Castle. Upon their deaths, the entire property was then donated to the Betsey Mills Corporation, which completed its final repairs.

The Castle opened for tours as a historical house museum in 1994. At that time, the Castle was initially furnished with antiques from the Bosleys, as well as donations of historical furniture from other Marietta families. Since then, however, a number of items relating to the various owners of the Castle have been donated to the museum and are now on display. Besides museum tours, the Castle also provides a number of educational and cultural offerings, including school and scout programs, history and archaeology summer camps, cemetery and historically-themed programs, and cultural bus trips. Today they honor the legacy of the Castle and its former residents while providing opportunities to learn of Marietta's connection to significant local, state, and national events.

SOMETHING DELICIOUS FROM
OUR WAYFARERS INN FRIENDS

Winnie's Famous Blueberry-Lemon Buttermilk Muffins

Makes 12 medium muffins

2¼ cups all-purpose flour, divided

1 cup sugar, divided

½ teaspoon salt

2 teaspoons baking powder

1 teaspoon baking soda

1½ cup fresh or frozen blueberries

grated zest of 1 lemon

1 tablespoon lemon juice

1 cup buttermilk

1 teaspoon vanilla

1 large egg

4 tablespoons butter, melted and cooled slightly

turbinado sugar, optional

Preheat oven to 350 degrees.

In a medium bowl, sift together 2 cups of the flour, ¾ cup of the sugar, salt, baking powder, and baking soda. Stir to mix, and set aside.

In a small bowl, toss the blueberries with the lemon zest, lemon juice, ¼ cup of the sugar, and ¼ cup of the flour. Set aside.

Pour the buttermilk and vanilla into a large measuring cup. Vigorously beat in the egg and the melted butter.

245

Make a well in the dry ingredients and pour the wet ingredients into the well. Stir quickly to incorporate, taking care to not overmix. The batter will not be smooth. Just before all the ingredients are combined, fold in the blueberry mixture and stir quickly to distribute the blueberries evenly throughout the batter.

Spoon the batter into a paper-lined muffin pan, sprinkle with turbinado sugar (optional), and bake for 20–25 minutes or until golden brown.

Read on for a sneak peek of another exciting book
in the Secrets of Wayfarers Inn series!

ALL THE INN'S A STAGE
by Roseanna M. White

Marietta Ohio
May 20, 1861

Prudence Willard sidestepped another pedestrian hurrying by and clutched her shopping basket tighter. There was much to do on this Monday morning, to be sure, and it seemed many of her neighbors had not yet learned the old adage that haste made waste. What was everyone's hurry today?

"It's the *Gilded Palace!*"

The excited shout, delivered almost directly in her ear as an adolescent boy jostled by her, seemed to be aimed at someone across the street, but it might as well have been a hammerblow directly to her heart. Her feet stopped, her throat tightened, and she couldn't convince her breath to fill her chest.

They were back. Ten years later, they were back. Prudence's mind swam. They'd thought the worst, she and Jason. Feared it. Accepted it. Mourned it.

But they were back.

The boy across the street ran over to his friend, now a few steps ahead of her. "Are they doing a show? I hope it's not Shakespeare. Though Ma will only let me go if it *is*."

"Bet they'll be announcing it. Might even have papers for us to hand out—Jimmy said he got to do that last time. They paid him two whole pennies for it."

The prospect of a paying job was apparently enough enticement to spur the youths onward at a reckless pace.

Prudence sucked in a breath and forced her own feet onward, more sedately. She had errands to finish. Then the mending and ironing to do. She hadn't time to scurry down to the docks with the rest of Marietta to discover if the *Gilded Palace* had come to do another show. And even if she did, there was no guarantee that Virgil was still with the company—or that the same company still owned the boat.

But the mere thought of him being in town made her decide that she didn't really need that new spool of thread today, after all. Next week would be soon enough. After a wagon lumbered by, she crossed the street, her feet aimed for home. She had to be the one to tell Jason, before someone else could mention it in his hearing.

"Prudence? Is that you, all grown up?"

The voice halted her just as she was cutting down an alleyway. It had been a decade since she'd heard it, it was true. But one didn't forget the voice of the person responsible for the maiming of the man one loved. Ever so slowly, she turned to face him. "Virgil Sullivan. Thee has finally returned."

Janice Eastman hummed the final notes of "'Tis So Sweet to Trust in Jesus" as she snipped the thread, freeing the shimmering fabric from her sewing machine. She held up the costume, shook it out, and smiled. Turned out pretty well, if she did say so herself.

"Hey, Janice. Have a minute?"

Janice stood, holding up the silver flapper-style dress as Tess walked into Janice's sitting/sewing room. "What do you think?"

Tess Wallace drew near with a smile significantly dimmer than usual. She nodded, even reached out to run appreciative fingers down the side of the dress, but her smile didn't brighten. "Beautiful, as expected. But..."

Janice lifted her brows. "But what?"

Tess sighed. "But all this effort might be wasted. I'm not sure the show will go on."

Janice laughed because her business partner and longtime friend *must* be joking. "Right. In all the years I've known Heidi

Ingram, she has not *once* cancelled a performance." On the contrary, when the theater teacher put on a show at the high school, everyone in town knew they could count on it being fantastic. It was why Janice, Tess, and the third member of their triad, LuAnn Sherrill, hadn't had any qualms about hosting the debut of Heidi's new enterprise. The Wayfarers Inn would make the perfect backdrop for her traveling murder mystery dinner theater. Plus, it would mean a weekend of guaranteed revenue for the inn.

Tess crossed her arms over her middle and surveyed the growing rack of costumes that Janice had designed and sewn for the event. It had been fun, being the costume department again. She'd done it countless times for the high school theater department before she retired, and frankly, she'd missed it.

Tess shook her head. "I'm sure if this were another high school or community production that didn't have to actually earn money, it would go off without a hitch. But this is a business, and I've been monitoring the ticket sales."

Janice grinned and slid the silver dress onto a hanger. Tess, the business mind of their inn, had been doing more than *monitoring* the ticket sales. She had set up an online system for purchasing them and had been taking any phone orders too, here at the inn. "I'm aware."

Tess stepped closer and lowered her voice, though they were the only two up here—aside from Tom and Huck, the cat and small dog currently curled up together in a patch of sunlight, snoozing. "She said she had to sell twenty tickets to break even, right? Preferably thirty. But she's only sold six. *Six!* And that was to her out-of-town family!"

The family that would be staying here for the weekend of the production. Janice let out a slow breath and did some quick calculations. Today was Tuesday, the seventh of May. The show was scheduled for the eighteenth. "She still has almost two weeks until the play."

"I know, but…" Tess stood back and shook her head, her eyes gleaming with that sad light that said *I know the numbers, and this is bad.* "I thought maybe you could talk to her. Make sure she knows that this needs to be addressed. Tickets have been on sale for a month, and for *no* orders to come in other than her own family is pretty depressing. I hate to see her and her team—and you—putting so much effort into the launch of a business that's just going to flop before it even gets started."

Janice put the hanger on the rack with a click of metal on metal. She didn't have to ask why Tess thought Janice should be the one to talk to Heidi. Heidi was Janice's friend, after all—they'd taught in the same school for years, and she'd been the one to suggest to Heidi that the inn could be a great venue for her new traveling theater's debut run. It had to be a hit, to show other businesses in town how profitable it could be for them to hire the theater company for their own special events.

She turned back to Tess with pursed lips. "All right. I'll talk to her when she comes by this afternoon to work on setup."

Tess's smile looked even tighter than it had when she'd come in. "She's here now, down in the library. That's why I came to find you."

With only one longing look at the shimmering blue fabric waiting on her worktable, ready to be turned into another 20s-era costume, Janice drew in a bolstering breath and headed for the door. "This ought to be fun."

"Now." Tess patted her shoulder. "Just put on your pastor's wife face. Kind and encouraging but no-nonsense."

Janice had certainly perfected said face over the years, before Lawrence died and made that part of her life obsolete. Thank the Lord that He gave her and Tess and LuAnn the idea for turning this old building back into an inn, or she didn't know how she'd be occupying her days now.

She and Tess walked together to the stairs and started down from their fourth-floor living quarters, all the way to the ground floor of Wayfarers Inn. Had they turned right at the bottom of the sweeping central staircase, they would have entered the soup café—closed after the lunch crowd had left—and then the kitchen. But instead they turned to the left, toward the parlor and library area, where the baby grand piano gleamed in the afternoon light, begging her to come and tickle its ivories.

Maybe she'd find some time later, before she went back to her sewing.

Assuming there was a point to going back to her sewing. She pasted on a smile that she hoped looked a little brighter than Tess's and strode into the room, toward the shelves where she spotted Heidi's golden-blond hair pulled back in a rare ponytail.

Janice stopped short when she saw the black T-shirt and jeans her friend wore. Usually, Heidi decked herself out in the closest thing to high fashion a fifty-year-old high school teacher could reasonably get away with. "Hi, Heidi."

At the greeting, Heidi spun, cables in her hands and a wide smile on her face. The day's makeup still adorned her face, complete with long lashes that Janice always suspected were fake...not that she'd ever dared to ask.

"Janice, hey! You're just in time. I could use an extra set of hands, and Leila's still a few minutes away."

Janice couldn't keep from bristling at the name. When she'd realized that Leila Johnson was on Heidi's cast, she'd taken her friend aside and asked if that was a good idea, knowing Heidi would remember that Leila had been the suspected culprit behind a particularly mean-spirited prank in Janice's classroom during her last year of teaching. Heidi had assured her Leila was all sweetness and talent. And no one had ever *proven* she'd been the one to sabotage each and every one of Janice's sewing machines.

She ought to give the girl the benefit of the doubt. She *would*. And so she covered the bristling with a smile. "What do you need me to do?"

"Could you hold these cables in place here while I run the other ends up along the top of the bookshelves?" Heidi motioned with her head toward the stepladder set up a few feet away.

"Sure." Janice cast a look at Tess—or tried to, but Tess was scurrying away. Maybe she'd heard the phone ring. Tucking a curl behind her ear, Janice crouched down to anchor the black cables on the floor.

Heidi was really going all out, rigging special effects all over the inn for the performance. It would be quite a show...if anyone showed up to see it. Janice drew in a breath, gave herself a pep talk, and decided to get it over with. "You're sure Leila can be trusted?"

Or maybe put it off for just a minute more.

"Hmm? Oh." Heidi hooked the stepladder with a foot, dragged it closer, and climbed up. "Look, I know she was the most likely suspect for that sewing machine thing, given that she dropped your class the day before. But seriously, Janice, she's a sweetheart. I don't think she did it. And even if she did, that was three years ago. Kids change a lot between freshman and senior years."

"Yeah, I know." Janice had certainly seen that plenty of times in her years of teaching. She held the cables still against a tug and made it a point not to peer around the bookcase at her friend. "As long as you're sure."

"I'm sure. She's a great kid. Very talented."

At texting, anyway. The other night when she had come over with the rest of Heidi's cast, she hadn't once put her phone down. Janice sighed and scolded herself for the mean-spirited thought. "I'm sure she is."

The bell at the front door jangled, which wouldn't have made her come to attention, except that LuAnn called out, "Get a load of this, guys!"

Janice didn't release the cables, but she did angle her body so she could see as LuAnn and Tess came into the room along with Brad Grimes carrying a large cardboard box in his arms.

Janice raised her eyebrows. "She putting you to work again, Brad?"

Their friend and Realtor grinned—and aimed it mostly at LuAnn, as usual. "I was chatting with LuAnn outside when Harry Olson dropped this off."

LuAnn looked absolutely giddy over whatever it was, going so far as to clap her hands. "Set it down anywhere, Brad, so we can open it."

Janice lifted her gaze toward Tess, who rolled her eyes and said, "Books."

Janice smiled. "Ah. That explains the craziness."

LuAnn was their resident literature and history buff, having just retired last year from her career as an English teacher.

The box certainly looked historical, which was a kind way of saying it was ready to fall apart. Janice asked the obvious question. "Why did Harry drop off a box of books?"

LuAnn didn't peel her eyes off the box as Brad lowered it gingerly to the floor. "He said some people were clearing out their attic and came across it, brought it to the antique mall. He has a hard time moving books but took them when he saw that they were all from Riverfront House."

Well, that did make them more interesting. They'd found plenty of things that had belonged to the original hotel in this building, but never books.

Tess leaned closer to peek inside. "How did he know they came from here?"

Brad opened the box, and LuAnn pulled out a book. She flipped through the first few pages. "My guess would be this

'Property of Riverfront House Hotel' stamp on the title page."

Heidi chuckled and continued tucking cables along the top of the shelf. "That's a good indicator. And hey, LuAnn, I wanted to thank you for your edits on my script. They were great!"

That actually pulled LuAnn's gaze off the book in her hand. "Oh, I'm glad you thought so. I was a little leery of suggesting such big changes to your plot, but…"

"No, I'm glad you did. It makes it so much more compelling. I already emailed the update to the cast. Dempsey won't be too happy that her part has shrunk, but I'll promise her a bigger role in next month's production."

Janice exchanged a glance with Tess, who lifted her brows. Her question was clear. *Did you talk to her yet?*

Janice gave her a sheepish shrug and rolled her eyes toward LuAnn and Brad and the interruption.

Heidi climbed down from the stepladder, moved it a few feet farther away, and climbed back up. "Almost done, Janice."

"No rush." She watched as LuAnn pulled out book after book, arranging them in piles that Janice couldn't detect the rhyme or reason for from this distance. Perhaps fiction and nonfiction. Or subject. Or condition. No doubt the nice ones would find a place on these very shelves beside which Janice was crouching, but some looked as battered as the box. "Anything good in there, Lu?"

"I haven't heard of most of them, but there are a few I recognize. A volume of Shakespeare, some poetry, that sort of thing." LuAnn pulled out an oversized but thin book and set it on the floor separate from the others. "I doubt that one would even fit on a shelf. Not upright, anyway."

Tess picked it up. "Mother Goose rhymes! How fun. I bet there are some good illustrations in here." She opened it up and then frowned. "Um..." She pulled out the pages. Just lifted them right out, as if they hadn't been bound in there at all.

Maybe they hadn't—the slender stack of yellowed paper wasn't quite the same size as the book and seemed to have a separate back cover of faded blue.

"What in the world?" LuAnn reached for the pages that Tess held out to her. "Odd. Definitely not Mother Goose. It looks like a script for a play. Part of one, anyway."

"A *what?*" As if LuAnn had spoken the magic word, Heidi jumped down from the ladder and flew to her side, all but dancing. "Can I see it? Can I? Please?"

LuAnn handed it over with a laugh. "Have at it."

"No front cover. I wonder what play it's for." Heidi flipped through a few pages, her eyes skimming over the lines. "I don't recognize it. Definitely just a fragment though. Looks like we don't have anything before page twenty-five."

Janice pushed herself up and joined the others.

Heidi closed the script and clasped it tight, eyes wide. "Whatever it is, it's surely a sign. The Marietta Murder Mystery Dinner Theater is going to be a huge success!"

Janice tried really, really hard not to meet Tess's gaze again. And though she failed, she was saved too many silent scoldings by the front door banging open.

"Move out of my way, Leila!"

Janice peered around Brad to see two young women entering, the older shoving the younger aside none too gently. Outrage marred her picture-perfect face.

She'd already met Heidi's star actress and had wondered more than once if the young woman realized that being a drama queen wasn't a necessary qualification for someone who wanted to make a career upon the stage.

Dempsey Keller brandished a few pages of her own—crisp and white and new. "This had better be a joke! I will *not* just stand by and let all my best lines be cut."

Janice glanced at LuAnn, who wisely edged behind Heidi.

There was really something to be said for sticking to her sewing machine and hot glue gun. She'd happily leave dealing with cranky actresses to someone else.

A Note from the Editors

We hope you enjoy Secrets of Wayfarers Inn, created by the Books and Inspirational Media Division of Guideposts, a nonprofit organization that touches millions of lives every day through products and services that inspire, encourage, help you grow in your faith, and celebrate God's love in every aspect of your daily life.

Thank you for making a difference with your purchase of this book, which helps fund our many outreach programs to military personnel, prisons, hospitals, nursing homes, and educational institutions. To learn more, visit Guideposts Foundation.org.

We also maintain many useful and uplifting online resources. Visit Guideposts.org to read true stories of hope and inspiration, access OurPrayer network, sign up for free newsletters, download free e-books, join our Facebook community, and follow our stimulating blogs.

To learn about other Guideposts publications, including the best-selling devotional *Daily Guideposts*, go to ShopGuideposts .org, call (800) 932-2145, or write to Guideposts, PO Box 5815, Harlan, Iowa 51593.

Sign up for the
Guideposts Fiction Newsletter
and stay up-to-date on the books you love!

guideposts·fiction
Inspiring reads chosen just for you!

What's New

Mysteries of Martha's Vineyard

Come to the shores of this quaint and historic island and dig in to a cozy mystery. When a recent widow inherits a lighthouse just off the coast of Massachusetts, she finds exciting adventures, new friends, and renewed hope.

On the quaint and historic island of Martha's Vineyard, just off the coast of Massachusetts, Priscilla comes face-to-face with adventure—one that includes rediscovered family, new friends, old homes, and head-scratching mysteries that crop up with surprising regularity. Learn More

Reader Favorite

Tearoom Mysteries

Take a quaint New England town... add some hidden treasures... a few suspicious characters... and a good measure of faith and friendship and you've brewed up Tearoom Mysteries!

Come explore this quaint village with its picturesque mountain lake surrounded by wild blueberry bushes, at your leisure. Like the people who come to Elaine and Jan's tearoom, you'll find yourself feeling relaxed. Learn More

From Our Editors

Sugarcreek Amish Mysteries

Sit back and enjoy a vacation for your soul with Sugarcreek Amish Mysteries. These well-written stories of the strong bond that develops between two women of vastly different backgrounds and traditions will tug at your heartstrings and provide hours of entertainment, intrigue, and wonder. In addition to Cheryl's keen insight and excellent riddle solving ability, you'll love experiencing Naomi's proverbial Amish wisdom and exploring her down-to-earth faith. Learn More

A perfect blend of faith, family, and fun!

You'll get sneak peeks of new releases, recommendations from other Guideposts readers, and special offers just for you . . .
and it's FREE!

Just go to Guideposts.org/Newsletters today to sign up.

Guideposts®

Visit Guideposts.org/Shop or call (800) 932-2145

Find more inspiring fiction in these best-loved Guideposts series!

Tearoom Mysteries Series

Mix one stately Victorian home, a charming lakeside town in Maine, and two adventurous cousins with a passion for tea and hospitality. Add a large scoop of intriguing mystery and sprinkle generously with faith, family, and friends, and you have the recipe for *Tearoom Mysteries.*

Sugarcreek Amish Mysteries

Be intrigued by the suspense and joyful "aha" moments in these delightful stories. Each book in the series brings together two women of vastly different backgrounds and traditions, who realize there's much more to the "simple life" than meets the eye.

Mysteries of Martha's Vineyard

What does Priscilla Latham Grant, a Kansas farm girl know about hidden treasure and rising tides, maritime history and local isle lore? Not much—but to save her lighthouse and family reputation, she better learn quickly!

Mysteries of Silver Peak

Escape to the historic mining town of Silver Peak, Colorado, and discover how one woman's love of antiques helps her solve mysteries buried deep in the town's checkered past.

To learn more about these books,
visit Guideposts.org/Shop